MIGHTY MORPHIN POWER RANGERS

ALL FEAR THE PHARAOH

by Neo Edmund

Penguin Young Readers Licenses
An Imprint of Penguin Random House

PENGUIN YOUNG READERS LICENSES
An Imprint of Penguin Random House LLC

™ and © 2018 SCG Power Rangers LLC. Power Rangers and all related logos, characters, names,
and distinctive likenesses thereof are the exclusive property of SCG Power Rangers LLC.
All Rights Reserved. Used Under Authorization. Published by Penguin Young Readers Licenses,
an imprint of Penguin Random House LLC, 345 Hudson Street, New York, New York 10014.
Printed in the USA.

Cover illustration by Patrick Spaziante.

ISBN 9781524784751   10 9 8 7 6 5 4 3 2 1

MIGHTY MORPHIN
POWER RANGERS

ALL FEAR THE
PHARAOH

Chapter 1

In the lobby of the Angel Grove History Museum, Trini Kwan stood looking up in awe at the fossilized skeleton of a sabertooth tiger. The prehistoric beast stood poised to attack, perched on its hind legs, its mouth full of razor-sharp teeth open. The awesome sight reminded Trini of the many times she'd piloted the mighty robotic Sabertooth Tiger Dinozord into battle against the evil forces of Rita Repulsa.

"Ms. Kwan, don't tell me you're daydreaming again," said an elderly lady with a shrill voice.

Trini looked back and saw the short and slender woman approaching. She wore a sparkling plum-purple dress with matching cowboy boots. A sash hung from her shoulder, decorated with over one hundred Angel Scout merit badges. Her name was Ms. Gertrude, the highest-ranking Angel Scout leader in Angel Grove.

"Ms. Gertrude, I wasn't daydreaming," Trini said

with a nervous crack in her voice. "I was just looking at the—"

"Excuses, excuses," Ms. Gertrude interrupted. "When I was your age, I had more discipline in my pinky finger than kids today have in their entire noggins."

Trini wanted to speak up in disagreement. She wanted to tell Ms. Gertrude that in school she earned straight As and had an outstanding attendance record. She wanted to tell her how she often organized community-service events. She also wanted to tell Ms. Gertrude how she had worked so hard to become a highly skilled martial artist. Of the many things Trini could have said to defend herself, experience had taught her that disagreeing with Ms. Gertrude would only make things worse.

"Sorry, ma'am. It won't happen again," Trini said.

Ms. Gertrude began to write notes on a clipboard. "Be sure that it doesn't. If you hope to pass the Angel Scout leadership exam, you must go above and beyond. Those bright-eyed young scouts will be looking to you for leadership and guidance," she said, then pointed toward the museum's main entrance. "Speaking of which, here they come now."

Trini smiled brightly as the young Angel Scouts entered the lobby. They were all between eight and ten years old and wore matching purple skirts with decorated sashes over white T-shirts. Their gleaming excitement reminded Trini of the many great adventures she had gone on when she was an Angel Scout. The chance to become one of their trusted leaders was just as important to Trini as her duties as the Yellow Power Ranger.

As the scouts approached, Trini was delighted to see her cousin Silvia was among them. "I didn't know you had joined the scouts," Trini said, giving her cousin a loving hug.

Silvia smiled and shrugged. "At first I didn't want to, but after hearing your stories about how great it all is, I thought I'd give it a try."

"I think it's a great thing that you did. I'm going to make sure you have so much fun, you'll wish you had joined a long time ago," Trini said.

Ms. Gertrude glared at Trini over her clipboard. "Watch yourself, Ms. Kwan. Favoritism will not be tolerated."

"I didn't mean it like that," Trini said assuredly. "It's just that I've been trying for a long time to get my cousin to join. Besides, you told me that recruiting is a very important part of a scout leader's job."

Ms. Gertrude reluctantly nodded in agreement. "Fine. I'll award you one bonus point for the new recruit." She marked down a point on her clipboard.

For the next two hours, Trini led the scouts through the various halls of the museum. She had spent nearly a week beforehand studying the many exhibits so she would be able to give the scouts the best possible learning experience. They saw art and science exhibits. Weapons and armor from various time periods. Even old computers from the early age of technology. Along the way, Trini tried her best to impress Ms. Gertrude, but somehow she managed to lose more points than she earned.

Just when Trini thought things couldn't get any worse, a towering brute stumbled into their path. He had lanky limbs and was wrapped in bandages from head to toe, like a mummy. His musty odor made him smell like he had crawled out of a tomb after a thousand years of slumber.

The mummy glared down at Trini and the scouts. "Welcome to the Tomb of the Griffin Pharaoh. The master has decreed that you all be put to death."

Chapter 2

The mummy extended its lanky arms wide and let out a roar. Even standing hunched forward, it towered over Trini by two feet. Silvia and the Angel Scouts screeched fearfully and scurried behind Trini for safety.

Trini, having fought in many battles, was not so easily shaken. With fearless eyes, she glared up at the menacing brute. "Back off, you creeper!"

The mummy snickered. "How could such a puny mortal possibly stand against my great strength?"

Trini took a fighting stance. "You put one hand on these girls, you'll find out I'm not so puny."

The mummy flinched nervously and took a big step backward. "Easy, it's just a game."

"What do you mean, 'a game'?" Trini asked, feeling quite confused.

Ms. Gertrude stepped between Trini and the mummy. "It means he is an actor."

Trini looked around the hall. Several other

mythical Egyptian creatures were lurking among the crowd. There was a golden sphinx, a catlike creature, a man-size scorpion, and a serpopard, which was a strange creature that resembled a leopard with the head and extra-long neck of a sea serpent.

Ms. Gertrude shook her head disapprovingly and wrote more notes on her clipboard. "As you can see, Ms. Kwan, they are merely performers in costumes."

Feeling foolish, Trini lowered her fist. "I'm so sorry," she said to the mummy. "I was just trying to protect the girls."

"You're not completely to blame," the mummy said. "I must admit I do look quite terrifying in this getup." He then ambled away.

Silvia took Trini's hand. "Don't feel bad. I think you were very brave."

The other Angel Scouts agreed wholeheartedly.

Ms. Gertrude grumbled. "Fine. I'll give you one bonus point for bravery and subtract one for poor judgment. Now can we just move along with the tour?"

Trini led the scouts around the hall, showing them the many amazing artifacts that had been unearthed in the Egyptian desert. There were stone tablets with strange writings. Weapons and armor once used by great warriors. Jeweled crowns worn by the emperors and empresses of the ancient world. Of the many amazing artifacts to be seen, all paled in comparison to a golden statue that reigned tall in the center of the hall.

"They called him the Griffin Pharaoh," Trini said as they approached the statue.

The girls looked up at the statue, awestruck.

From the waist down, the mighty winged creature had the legs and body of a lion. From the waist up, he had the muscular chest and arms of a man and the head of a mighty bird. In his talon-like hands, he gripped a golden staff with sparkling jewels embedded in the hilt.

Trini began to read from a plaque at the base of the statue. "According to legend, the Griffin Pharaoh was a tyrant who conquered the ancient world by imprisoning in mystical urns all those who opposed him. He then used his cyclone staff to send the urns soaring away to the far corners of the earth. Each urn was protected by a guardian beast that would attack anyone who dared to come near it. Once all his enemies were defeated, the Griffin Pharaoh used his hypnotic powers to turn everyone into mindless servants. It is believed that he once had hundreds of mystical urns, but now only five of the relics remain."

Trini and the scouts stepped up for a closer look at the five urns. They were three feet tall and forged from glossy black metal. Each had the image of a guardian beast carved into the side: a sphinx, a mythical cat, a mummy, a scorpion, and a serpopard.

Silvia raised a hand. "So how was the Griffin Pharaoh defeated?"

Trini looked again at the plaque. "That part of the legend doesn't seem to be included here."

"I bet he was beaten by the Power Rangers," Silvia said. "They fight monsters like him all the time."

Another scout named Daisy shook her head. "There were no Power Rangers back then."

"There were so," Silvia said. "Isn't that right, Trini?"

Trini could have easily told them the answer, but she had a better idea in mind. "I think you should research the subject. It would be a great way to earn a Historical Research Merit Badge."

"Unless you're afraid you'll get proven wrong," Daisy teased.

"I'm not wrong, and I'm not afraid," Silvia said and then stomped away.

Daisy let out a screech and stormed off in the other direction.

"Girls, wait," Trini called out, but Silvia and Daisy were already gone.

"Not good at all," Ms. Gertrude said. She wrote more notes on her clipboard and strutted away.

Trini let out a long sigh, certain she had failed the first part of her leadership exam.

Chapter 3

In the darkest shadows of the dusty gray moon stood the palace of the villainous witch Rita Repulsa. Standing on the observation deck atop the tallest tower, a delinquent pair of aliens was spying on Trini through Rita's extreme long-range telescope. One was called Squatt, a short and pudgy creature with a big head and huge teeth. The other alien was a lanky apelike creature with blue skin named Baboo.

"Oh, this is too perfect," Baboo said diabolically. Peering through the telescope, he was able to see Trini at the Angel Grove History Museum, still looking at the statue of the Griffin Pharaoh. "That meddlesome Yellow Ranger just gave me a great idea of how we can do away with all the Rangers in one fell swoop."

"Let me see," Squatt said, trying to shove Baboo away from the telescope.

"Not now, you blubbering fool. I'm busy plotting," Baboo said, pushing Squatt hard enough to knock him flat onto his back end.

Finster, an intellectual gray-skinned alien with pointy ears and a long snout, stepped up behind Squatt and Baboo. "You two had better get away from Rita's telescope before she turns you into a pair of hairless newts."

Baboo raised a fist at Finster. "What Rita doesn't know won't hurt you. Get my meaning?"

Finster cowered nervously.

"It doesn't matter, anyway," Squatt said. "Rita is away on secret business, and she left us in charge until she gets back."

"She didn't tell me anything of the sort," Finster said skeptically.

"If she had told you, it wouldn't be a secret," said Squatt.

Finster glared at them through his thick glasses. "If it's a secret, then how did you two come to know about it?"

"Because she told us not to tell when she left, dummy," said Baboo.

"Anyway, we don't have time for boring questions," said Squatt. "We're busy plotting against the Power Rangers."

"Now if I could just remember what we're plotting," Baboo said, again looking through the telescope. This time he saw that Trini and the scouts were departing from the tomb of the Griffin Pharaoh. "Now I remember. We're going to bring that Griffin Pharaoh statue to life."

"What nonsense are you talking about now?" Finster asked, nudging Baboo aside and peering through the telescope. He saw a security guard turn off the lights. The Griffin Pharaoh looked even more frightening in the dark. "Oh my! He sure would make a formidable nemesis for those blasted Rangers."

"Then you'll help us?" Baboo asked.

"Yeah, will you?" asked Squatt. He scratched his head in confusion. "Wait, why do we want to bring the Griffin Pharaoh to life?"

Baboo smacked Squatt on the head. "So we can order him to trap the Power Rangers inside those urns and send them to the far reaches of the world, just like it says in the legend."

Finster considered this. "It does sound like a good plan, but Rita would be furious if she found out we were acting without her permission."

Baboo stared down at Finster. "We don't need

permission because Rita left us in charge."

Squatt grabbed Finster by his overalls. "And what we say goes, get it?"

"Okay, okay. Just get your brutish hands off me, and I'll help," Finster said, struggling to get away from Squatt. "Follow me to my laboratory, and I'll figure something out."

Squatt and Baboo raised their arms in victory.

"Rita is going to be so proud of us when she finds out we finally defeated the Power Rangers," Squatt said.

"She sure will, but first we got to do it, so let's get to it," Baboo said.

Finster led Squatt and Baboo down a dank and dreary stone corridor. They passed several iron cell doors, each with vicious creatures growling and grunting on the other side. They entered Finster's workshop. Clay molds of vicious monsters lined the wooden shelves. Flames blasted from the sides of his Monster-Matic oven in the far corner; he used the nefarious machine to bring his clay monsters to life.

Finster scurried over to an old metal chest in the corner and heaved open the top. The chest was filled to the brim with dusty jars and glass vials, all containing rare ingredients used in his many alchemic creations.

The bottles clinked and clanked as he searched. At the very bottom of the chest, he found a bottle full of black sand.

"I believe this will do the trick," Finster said.

Squatt snatched the bottle from Finster and took a closer look. "How is a jar of dirt going to help us?"

"Careful! That's very fragile," Finster said. He grabbed the bottle back from Squatt and held it up to the light, revealing that the sand grains were moving around as if they were alive. "This rare Nanosand can only be found on a tiny moon over a billion light-years away. It has the unique ability to turn any form of matter into a living being. Not only that, it will take on the personality of the Griffin Pharaoh, just as described in the legend."

"How?" Squatt asked, scratching his head in confusion.

Baboo shrugged. "Who cares how, as long as we can use him to trap the Power Rangers in his urns and send them so far away nobody will ever find them."

Squatt jumped around joyfully. "I can't wait to see the look on Rita's face when she finds out what we've done."

"This had better work," Finster said nervously. "If

we fail, the look on Rita's face will be the last thing we see before she blasts us into oblivion."

"You worry too much," said Squatt.

"What could possibly go wrong?" Baboo asked.

Squat and Baboo exchanged a victorious high five and then strutted away.

Chapter 4

At the Angel Grove Youth Center, the Angel Scouts were busy hosting a bake sale. Homemade cookies, cakes, and candies filled every inch of two large tables. A long line of buyers waited eagerly to support their cause.

At the same time, Trini and Ms. Gertrude oversaw a team of scouts who were performing a first-aid training seminar. Ernie, the jolly owner of the Youth Center, sat in a chair as the scouts wrapped his limbs in splints and bandages.

"Ernie, I can't thank you enough for letting us use the Youth Center today," Trini said.

"Anything to help the Angel Scouts," Ernie said gleefully. "And you're doing a great job. You should be proud, Trini."

Ms. Gertrude wrote notes on her clipboard. "I must admit the first-aid demonstration is a clever idea to boost interest in the bake sale, though I'm not keen on the amount of sugary snacks being offered for sale."

"Not to worry about that," Ernie said assuredly. "My juice bar is fully stocked with all the healthy choices anyone could ask for."

"Be that as it may, next time I expect to see healthier options, Ms. Kwan," said Ms. Gertrude.

Trini held back a frustrated sigh and instead nodded in agreement.

Ms. Gertrude wrote more notes on her clipboard and walked away.

Trini noticed Silvia sitting at a table on the far end of the room. She was working on a laptop and was gritting her teeth in irritation. A little concerned, Trini walked over to check on her.

"Everything okay, Silvia?" Trini asked.

"Not even close. I'm doing research on the Griffin Pharaoh, but I can't find anything useful on the Internet," Silvia grumbled.

Trini sat down next to her cousin. "I'm glad you're taking this project so seriously, but I think you'd have more fun helping out with the bake sale or wrapping Ernie up like a mummy with the other scouts."

"I guess so," Silvia said, closing her laptop.

"Anyway, I'll have to go to a library to finish my research, if libraries even exist anymore."

Trini giggled. "I'm pretty sure there are a few left. And if you want, I'll even go with you."

"You're the best cousin ever," Silvia said, hugging Trini. "Now let's go sell some cookies."

Trini and Silvia made their way back over to join the other scouts.

"Angel Scouts, you're all doing great work here," said Trini. "We've already raised more than enough money to pay for our big road trip this summer."

The Scouts cheered and applauded.

At the front door, a dimwitted pair of punks named Bulk and Skull strutted into the room. Skull was lanky, while Bulk was tall and pudgy. Both wore ripped jeans with leather jackets over grungy T-shirts.

Bulk salivated like a hungry dog when he saw there was a bake sale going on. "Do you see what I see?"

"You bet your double-wide rump I do," Skull said, licking his chops. "We gotta get us some of that yumminess."

Bulk and Skull raced over toward the table, pushing past the line to get to the front.

"Give us two of everything, and make it quick," Bulk demanded.

"We're hankering for some sugary treats, and we want 'em now," Skull said.

The scouts looked at one another, uncertain what to do.

"Don't worry, scouts. I've got this," Trini said, grinning a little. She picked up two large brownies. "These sure smell good. I bet you guys could eat a whole plateful."

"You know we could, so give me, give me," Skull said.

Bulk and Skull grabbed for the brownies, but Trini stepped away.

"Hey, what gives, Trini?" Bulk asked.

"Funny you should say 'gives,' because everyone here is giving donations to the Angel Scouts in exchange for the treats," Trini said.

Bulk crinkled his nose. "As in, like, give you money?"

"We've never given anyone anything in our lives," Skull protested.

"There's never a better time to start than right now," Trini said. "Your generous donations will help to pay for the scouts to go on camping trips like the one we're going on tomorrow."

"Why should we care about a bunch of goody-goody scouts going on a camping trip?" Bulk asked.

Trini shook her head in disbelief. "If I have to explain it to you, then you'll never get it, so I have another idea. We need some more volunteers for the first-aid demonstration. If you two agree to help out, you can each have two free items."

Bulk and Skull looked at her skeptically.

"And what would we have to volunteer to do?" Bulk asked.

"All you have to do is just sit in the chairs. The scouts will do the rest," said Trini.

"Heck, I'll do that," said Skull. "We just sit around doing nothing for free all the time."

Bulk and Skull strutted over to the first-aid demonstration area and sat down in two chairs. The scouts got right to work, wrapping Bulk's and Skull's limbs in bandages and splints. It took only a brief moment before Bulk and Skull began to fidget around impatiently.

"How long is this going to take?" Bulk grumbled. "We're hungry and we want some sugary goodness."

"Yeah, let's put this demonstration into overdrive," Skull demanded.

The scouts shrugged and began to work faster, passing the rolls of bandages to one another as quickly as they could. Bulk and Skull continued demanding that the girls speed up.

The scouts began to get annoyed and started to wrap the bandages around Bulk's and Skull's eyes. Finally, the scouts turned Bulk's and Skull's chairs back-to-back and used the bandages to bind the duo together so they were unable to move.

"Bulk, what's happening? I can't see anything," Skull squealed in a panic.

"All I want to know is when we're getting our brownies," Bulk said.

The girls giggled and exchanged high fives.

Trini turned around and did her best to hold back a giggle when she saw what had happened. "Scouts, I think you might have gone a little too far there."

Ms. Gertrude, furious, came stomping over. "What in tarnation is going on here?"

Trini tried to hide her smirking grin. "Ms. Gertrude, please don't be angry. The scouts were just having a little fun with Bulk and Skull."

"Angel Scouts do not engage in unruly mischief. Unwrap these boys this instant," Ms. Gertrude demanded.

The scouts quickly unraveled the bandages, freeing Bulk and Skull. The two leaped up and looked around in anger and confusion.

"You think that's funny?" Bulk asked. "You just wait. We'll show you what's funny."

"Yeah, we'll learn you what's funny, real good," said Skull.

They each grabbed a plate of brownies and then stomped away.

Ms. Gertrude shook her head in disappointment. "Ms. Kwan, you've set a poor example for the scouts. A poor example, indeed."

Trini considered this and nodded. "You're right. It won't happen again."

Ms. Gertrude wrote notes on her clipboard and walked away.

A familiar chime sounded from the communicator strapped to Trini's wrist. Jason, the Red Ranger and leader of the Power Rangers, was calling her. This usually meant trouble was brewing in Angel Grove.

Trini hurried out of the front door of the

Youth Center. She looked around to assure herself that nobody was watching, then spoke into her communicator. "What's up, Jason?"

"Rita's no-good Putty Patrollers are terrorizing the security guards at the Angel Grove History Museum."

"What could they possibly be up to at the museum?" Trini asked.

"I don't know, but the other Rangers and I are already on the way. We need you to meet us there right away," Jason said urgently.

Trini looked around to make sure nobody was watching. "It's Morphin Time!" she said, then reached behind her back and pulled out her Power Morpher. "Sabertooth Tiger Dinozord!" she shouted.

In a flickering flash, she morphed into the mighty Yellow Ranger and then teleported to the museum.

Chapter 5

The instant the Yellow Ranger teleported into the Angel Grove History Museum, the fight was on. Dozens of gray-skinned monstrous brutes called Putty Patrollers were swarming all around. The other Rangers were already engaged in battle and were greatly outnumbered.

A Putty with fists raised and ready to strike raced toward the Yellow Ranger. She unleashed a flurry of kicks, knocking the clay creature into a wall. The impact caused a priceless porcelain vase to fall from a display and plummet toward the marble floor. Jason, the Red Ranger, raced over and caught the vase a second before impact.

"Thanks for the assist," the Yellow Ranger said, letting out a sigh of relief. "We've gotta get these clowns out of here before they trash the place."

"It would help if we knew what they're doing here to begin with," said the Red Ranger. He then turned to face off with another pair of Putty Patrollers.

"A little help, please," Zack, the Black Ranger, called out from nearby. He was being restrained by a half dozen Putty Patrollers.

The Yellow Ranger dashed his way to help, but a Putty leaped into her path. Another Putty Patroller grabbed her from behind and locked its arms around her waist. The Yellow Ranger jammed her elbow into the Putty Patroller's gut, forcing it to release her. She grabbed its arm and thrust it with all her might into the Putty blocking her path. The force of the impact caused both Putties to burst into a thousand bits of clay.

The Yellow Ranger noticed that Kimberly, the Pink Ranger, was surrounded by more Putty Patrollers than she could handle on her own. She then looked over and saw that Billy, the Blue Ranger, was in the same predicament. Things weren't looking good for the Red Ranger, either, as he tried to take on a dozen of the gray brutes.

The Yellow Ranger knew that there was no way to help them all. She needed a plan of attack, and she needed one quickly. "Alpha 5, do you hear me?" the Yellow Ranger shouted into her helmet's communicator.

"Aye-yi-yi, are you okay, Trini?" Alpha 5 replied.

"I am for now, but I don't know what to do," the Yellow Ranger said, gasping to catch her breath. "There are way too many Putties for us to handle."

The voice of the Rangers' mentor, Zordon, came through on the communicator. "Trini, I know you want to help the other Rangers, but there is another pressing matter that needs your attention. We have spotted Squatt and Baboo heading toward the museum hall called the Tomb of the Griffin Pharaoh."

"Whatever those two are up to, it can only add up to bad news for Angel Grove," said Alpha 5.

The Red Ranger looked at the Yellow Ranger. "Stopping Squatt and Baboo is more important," he shouted. "Don't worry about us. We've got this."

The Yellow Ranger nodded reluctantly and then took off running.

For the next few minutes, the Yellow Ranger raced through the museum. She looked back and was startled to see several Putty Patrollers chasing after her, and they were gaining quickly. She dashed down a staircase and then rounded a tight corner, nearly slipping on the smooth marble floor. Many of the Putty Patrollers slipped and then crashed head-on into a wall.

The Yellow Ranger reached the towering archway leading into the Tomb of the Griffin Pharaoh. Despite her best effort, several of the Putty Patrollers were hot on her heels. When she entered the hall, she saw Squatt and Baboo standing near the statue of the Griffin Pharaoh.

Squatt was struggling to pry open the lid on the bottle of Nanosand.

"Hurry up, you dunce, that meddlesome Yellow Ranger is coming," Baboo said.

"I'm trying, but the top is stuck," said a frustrated Squatt.

The Yellow Ranger had no idea what was inside the bottle, but she was certain that she had to stop them from opening it. Taking a mighty leap through the air, she soared toward the dimwitted duo. She extended her arm forward, hoping against hope that she could snatch the bottle away from them before it was too late.

"Just give it to me," Squatt said, grabbing the bottle from Baboo. He flung the bottle with all his might at the Griffin Pharaoh statue. The brittle glass shattered into shards on impact. The Nanosand scattered all around the base of the statue.

The Yellow Ranger soared past Squatt and Baboo. She hit the floor and dive-rolled to her feet. Her effort to foil their evil plan had failed.

Chapter 6

The Yellow Ranger watched in terror as the grains of Nanosand rapidly multiplied and swarmed over the statue of the Griffin Pharaoh. In mere seconds, the tiny organisms covered every inch of the statue from its head to its toes. An ominous glowing white light ignited as the grains began to burrow into its golden surface.

"What have you two done?" the Yellow Ranger asked.

Squatt and Baboo broke into triumphant laughter.

Putty Patrollers swarmed into the hall and surrounded the Yellow Ranger. Before she could react, they grabbed her arms and held her tight. She flailed and kicked with all her might, trying to break their grip, but it was hopeless.

The Nanosand started to transform the golden surface of the Griffin Pharaoh statue into living flesh. The statue's arms began to sway around slowly, followed by the legs. The chest expanded and contracted as air flowed in and out of its massive lungs. The statue was coming to life, and the Yellow Ranger couldn't do anything to stop it.

The Griffin Pharaoh's eyes snapped open. He looked around the hall in dazed confusion. "After five thousand years of darkness, I live. But how can this be?"

Squatt waved at him. "You can thank us for that."

"We brought you to life to destroy the Power Rangers," said Baboo.

The Griffin Pharaoh glared at them. "I have no foes called the Power Rangers."

"You do now," Squatt said, pointing at the Yellow Ranger, who was still struggling to break free from the clutches of the Putty Patrollers.

The Griffin Pharaoh wailed with thunderous laughter. "Your power is nothing compared to mine. I will prove that to you now," he said, extending an arm and holding out his cyclone staff.

The golden rod began to spin around and around in the Griffin Pharaoh's hand like a huge fan, blasting gusts of wind toward the Yellow Ranger. The Putty Patrollers lost their grip on her and were sent soaring away. One after another, they slammed into the walls and pillars, so hard that they were destroyed on impact.

Squatt and Baboo held on to a pillar to save themselves from being blown away.

"We better get out of here, or we'll be the next to get splattered," said Squatt.

"What about the Yellow Ranger?" Baboo asked.

"The Griffin Pharaoh can handle her," Squatt replied.

In a flash, they teleported away.

The wind now blasted so hard, the Yellow Ranger's feet began to slide backward on the marble floor.

"And now, Yellow Ranger, you will be destroyed." The Griffin Pharaoh thrust his staff forward and hurtled a burst of glowing energy at the Yellow Ranger. The shock wave sent her flailing through the air, head-on into the far wall. She toppled to the ground and collapsed. The force of the impact caused her to de-morph and turn back into her normal form.

Spinning with dizziness, Trini looked up and saw the other Rangers were racing into the hall. She tried to call out and warn them about the dangerous power of the Griffin Pharaoh's cyclone staff, but she was too disoriented to speak. She could only watch as her fellow Rangers prepared to engage him in battle.

The Griffin Pharaoh glared at the Rangers. "You don't look so mighty to me."

The Red Ranger raised a fist. "I was just going to say the same thing about you."

All at once, the four Rangers attacked the Griffin Pharaoh, unleashing a dazzling assault of kicks and punches. The Griffin Pharaoh proved to be much too tough and easily blocked each of their valiant strikes. He then counterattacked with a ruthless barrage of his blows.

"You pathetic weaklings don't deserve to do battle against my greatness," the Griffin Pharaoh said mockingly. "For such insolence, you must now pay the price."

Trini knew exactly what the Griffin Pharaoh was planning to do. She tried to warn the Rangers, but her voice was still stifled and weak.

The Griffin Pharaoh pointed his staff at the urns sitting nearby. The tops of four of the five urns hinged open. A cloudy black shadow, in the form of a hand, arose from inside each of the urns. The shadow-hands swarmed toward the Rangers and snatched them up.

"Zordon, we have to help them," Trini muttered into her communicator.

"I'm afraid there is nothing we can do," Zordon replied. "You must escape before you fall to the same fate."

The mystical shadow-hands dragged the Rangers toward the urns. The four valiant heroes desperately tried to break free, but there would be no escape for them. The shadow-hands caused the Rangers to shrink and then shoved them into the urns.

Finally, the urns changed colors to match the Rangers now trapped within.

"Trini, you can delay no longer. You must teleport out of there now," Zordon insisted.

Trini nodded reluctantly. "I hate to leave them, but I know you're right," she said, then tapped her communicator. A distorted yellow light flickered around her then faded away. She tapped the communicator again, with the same result. "Zordon, something is wrong with my communicator," she said.

"Aye-yi-yi! There's some sort of interference," Alpha 5 yelped. "Hold on, Trini, I'll get you out of there."

Nearby, the Griffin Pharaoh laughed wickedly.

"Now to send you Rangers so far away nobody will ever be able to find you," he said. His cyclone staff began to spin rapidly. Tornado-like gusts of wind picked up the four urns and carried them toward the ceiling. Trini watched in hopeless terror as the urns crashed through a skylight and soared off in four different directions.

"Now to deal with that Yellow Ranger," the Griffin Pharaoh said. He turned and saw Trini standing on the far end of the room. "Peasant girl, where did the Yellow Ranger go?"

Trini was relieved that he hadn't seen her de-morph, so he didn't know that she was the Yellow Ranger. A yellow light began to flicker around her. Alpha 5 had come through. "Figure it out yourself, freak face," she said and then teleported away.

Chapter 7

In the main control room of the Power Rangers' Command Center, Trini typed a series of commands into one of the many blinking computer consoles. A three-dimensional image of her wrist-communicator came up on-screen, revealing the complex inner workings of the device.

The communicator itself sat upon a metal tray inside a transparent diagnostic chamber. Laser scanners beamed across the metallic surface of the communicator, looking for any defects that might have prevented Trini from teleporting during her battle with the Griffin Pharaoh.

Alpha 5, the Command Center's cybernetic caretaker, scurried from one blinking computer console to another, flicking switches and pushing buttons. On her console screen, Trini eagerly watched the digitized image of the communicator. After a brief moment, the display flashed green, indicating the device was in perfect working order.

"Very strange," Alpha 5 said, shrugging. "I can't find any reason that you were unable to teleport during the battle. Are you sure you were pushing the right button, Trini? You were pretty dizzy after taking that hit that caused you to de-morph."

Trini pressed a hand to her head, still feeling a little dazed. "I guess anything is possible, but I really think there's more to it than that."

Zordon, an ancient galactic sage trapped in a time warp, looked down at Trini from inside a glass energy chamber that served as his link to the Command Center. "During your battle with the Griffin Pharaoh, I detected several bursts of a rare form of power called nanotronic energy. It is possible that this nanotronic energy caused your communicator to malfunction," he said.

Trini had never heard of nanotronic energy, and had there been more time, she would have asked Zordon for an explanation. At the moment, far more pressing concerns were weighing on her mind. She took her communicator from the diagnostic chamber and strapped it to her wrist. "Well, it seems to be working fine now, so we should start searching for the other Rangers right away," she said.

Zordon nodded. "Alpha 5 and I have already begun a search. Unfortunately, our scans have yet to reveal the location of the missing urns."

"Don't you worry, Trini," Alpha 5 said, flicking more switches on the console. "I won't stop working for a second until all the Rangers are located."

"Thank you, Alpha 5, but I can't just sit here doing nothing. It's bad enough that I ran away from the fight," Trini said shamefully.

"You cannot blame yourself for what was beyond your control," Zordon said. "Had you not fled when you did, you would have surely been captured as well."

"That could have been the end of the Power Rangers, forever," Alpha 5 said.

"I know you're right," Trini admitted regretfully. "I just don't understand how this even happened. Before today, the Griffin Pharaoh was just a character from an old myth. How could two idiots like Squatt and Baboo manage to bring his statue to life?"

"Based on the data we collected during your encounter with the Griffin Pharaoh, I believe they used a rare species of Nanosand found only on a moon in a distant nebula," Zordon said.

Alpha 5 brought up an image of the Griffin Pharaoh on a computer screen. Millions of the tiny Nanosand grains swarmed around his body. "Nanosand has the unique ability to turn matter into living flesh. The good news is the process of nano-solidification takes several days to complete."

Trini looked closer at the screen. "So right now the Griffin Pharaoh is still made of stone and gold. What happens after this nano-solidification is done?"

"I'm afraid the Griffin Pharaoh may become indestructible," Zordon said.

Trini paced nervously. "The Griffin Pharaoh is already too powerful for me to defeat on my own. We have to find the other Rangers to stand a chance against him."

"Alpha 5 and I will find them as soon as possible," Zordon said. "In the meantime, you should return to Angel Grove and continue your effort to become a leader of the Angel Scouts."

Trini shook her head. "How can I leave while the other Rangers are lost?"

"I know you want to help, but until the urns are located, there is little else you can do," Zordon said. "Never forget that becoming an Angel Scout leader is equally as important as your commitment to the Power Rangers."

"I'll contact you as soon as I have any new information," Alpha 5 said.

"You're right as always, Zordon. That doesn't make this any easier," Trini said. She reluctantly tapped her wrist-communicator and teleported away.

At the same time, the Griffin Pharaoh sat on Rita's golden throne in the Moon Palace. "This will make an excellent place for me to rule over the world. Or at least until I have enough slaves to build my new fortress."

Squatt and Baboo paced in a frantic panic.

"Are you crazy? You can't sit there," Baboo said.

"Only Queen Rita can sit on that throne," said Squatt.

The Griffin Pharaoh laughed. "If this Rita wishes to have it back, she will have to face me in battle. Until that time, you will all serve under my command." He looked at the Nanosand swarming on his arms. "And these strange creatures are still healing me, so I'm not going anywhere just yet."

Squatt raised a fist at the Griffin Pharaoh. "That's not how this is supposed to work. We brought you to life so that you could serve us."

"We order you to go back to Earth and destroy that meddlesome Yellow Ranger," said Baboo.

"You dare try to order me around. All will kneel before me, or all will be destroyed," the Griffin Pharaoh shouted. He raised his cyclone staff and blasted Squatt and Baboo with a gust of wind powerful enough to knock them to their knees.

Finster strutted into the room, carrying one of his clay monsters. He stopped in his tracks when he saw what was taking place. "What in the world is going on here?"

Baboo stumbled to his feet. "I'll tell you what's going on. This royal pain in the rump is trying to take over Rita's palace."

"And he won't listen to a thing we tell him," said Squatt.

Finster fidgeted nervously. "Oh dear, I worried that this could happen."

Squatt gave Finster a shove. "You better find a way to get the Griffin Pharaoh under control."

Baboo gave Finster an even harder shove. "And

you better make it happen before Rita gets back, or you'll be in big trouble."

Finster shook a fist in anger. "Don't blame me. This plan was your idea, not mine."

"Yeah, but it was your sand that brought the Griffin Pharaoh to life," said Baboo.

"Who do you think Rita is going to be madder at? Us or you?" Squatt asked.

The two aliens then strutted away.

Finster smacked a hand to his forehead. "How could I have been so foolish to listen to that pair of idiots?"

Chapter 8

The next morning, Trini rushed into a secluded area of Angel Grove Forest. She had spent the night tossing and turning, dreaming of the Griffin Pharaoh, and had overslept. She made a quick sprint down a dusty path toward the campground. Along the way, she tried to think up a believable excuse to explain to Ms. Gertrude why she was late, but upon reaching the campground, she realized even the best excuse in the world wasn't going to help. The scouts' campsite was already set up, a task Ms. Gertrude had put Trini in charge of overseeing.

"Trini!" Silvia called out gleefully and hurried over to greet her. "I was worried you got abducted by aliens or something."

Trini smiled at her cousin. "I didn't mean to be late. I just lost track of time."

"For two hours and twelve minutes," said Ms. Gertrude, from somewhere nearby. "That is the precise amount of time that you are late."

Trini looked around, but she couldn't see Ms. Gertrude. Silvia sighed and pointed upward. Trini looked up and was surprised to see Ms. Gertrude perched on a tree branch high above them. The woman was dressed in a gray safari outfit and glared down at them through a large pair of binoculars.

"Ms. Gertrude, what are you doing up there?" Trini asked.

"Bird-watching, of course," Ms. Gertrude said. She began to climb down. "When I was an Angel Scout, I completed the requirements for the Bird-Watching Merit Badge on three occasions. If you wonder why I would do such a thing, it is because I was dissatisfied with my performance on the first two attempts. I suppose that concept wouldn't make sense to one who takes her responsibilities so lightly."

Trini wanted to voice her disagreement with Ms. Gertrude, but she decided it was best not to argue. "I promise I won't be late again."

"See that you do not," Ms. Gertrude said, as she reached the ground. "Now without further delay, let us get this campout started. I assume you have an appropriate activity planned for the Artistic

Expression Merit Badge," she said, then blew a whistle.

The scouts hurried over and formed a line.

Trini took a calming breath before starting. "I think we're all going to have a great time this weekend. For our art project, we're going to make Maori-style masks, similar to the ones we saw at the museum."

The scouts looked at one another, uncertain what she was talking about.

"Remember, the exhibit had all sorts of interesting masks from Oceania," Trini said.

The scouts shrugged again.

Trini fidgeted nervously when she noticed Ms. Gertrude writing another note on her clipboard. "Anyway, for today's art project, we're going to be making our own masks. I want you all to give your mask a personality that represents you."

For the next few hours, Trini and the scouts created a dazzling assortment of colorful masks. Some looked silly and playful, while others were devious and even creepy in style. Trini did her best to oversee the activity with careful attention, and yet somehow she just couldn't seem to impress Ms. Gertrude.

As the setting sun gave way to night, the scouts built a crackling campfire. They wanted to roast marshmallows and tell spooky stories, but Ms. Gertrude overruled their plan, insisting that marshmallows were too sugary and scary tales would give them bad dreams. When the scouts tried to entertain themselves by singing campfire songs, Ms. Gertrude would only allow them to sing classics such as "Home on the Range," "Yankee Doodle," and "America the Beautiful."

By half past eight o'clock, Ms. Gertrude had fallen asleep and was snoring as loudly as a bear.

Trini tried to keep the scouts in an upbeat mood, but they soon became bored and restless.

"This is so boring," Silvia grumbled. "I wish we could just tell ghost stories."

The scouts all mumbled in agreement.

"So do I, but it's not up to me to decide," Trini said.

"But Ms. Gertrude is asleep," Silvia said, waving a hand in front of Ms. Gertrude's closed eyes. "She'll never even know."

"Just because we can get away with breaking a rule doesn't make it okay," Trini said. "Angel Scouts must always strive to be honest and true."

Silvia and the scouts half-heartedly mumbled in agreement.

Suddenly, the sound of crackling footsteps could be heard coming from the nearby bushes. Something was lurking in the shadows just beyond the edge of the campground. For a tense moment, Trini and the scouts listened in breathless silence. Again, they heard footsteps, this time followed by a bellowing growl and a vicious screech.

All at once the scouts screamed in terror.

Chapter 9

A furious growl. A savage grunt. A shrieking scream. The Angel Scouts huddled together in dreadful fear as the terrible sounds continued to come from the nearby shadows. Trini did her best to keep the girls calm, which wasn't easy because her own heart was racing with fear. As for Ms. Gertrude, she continued to snore like a wild beast.

After several moments had passed and the grunts and groans continued without pause, Trini started to feel suspicious of the source of the sounds. She signaled the girls to remain together and then crept over to a tree. Climbing with catlike agility, she hopped up to a high-hanging branch so she could get a bird's-eye view of the area. Just as she suspected, Bulk and Skull were hiding in the bushes. They were using an old electronic keyboard to create the terrible sounds.

Trini climbed back down the tree and hurried over

to the scouts. "It looks like a couple of wild animals have wandered into our campground. Fortunately, they're not dangerous, just obnoxious," she said to the wholehearted relief of the scouts. "I have an idea how we can scare them away."

As the fake growling and cackling continued, the scouts covered themselves in blankets and put on the masks they had created earlier in the day. They then stealthily made their way over to where Bulk and Skull were hiding.

"When I say go, we're going to jump out and make as much noise as we can," Trini whispered. Once the scouts were ready, she shouted, "GO!"

All at once, Trini and the scouts dashed around the tree, roaring and screeching. In the dark, they looked like a pack of wild monsters. Bulk and Skull were so startled that they wailed.

"We are the Were-Beasts of Angel Grove Forest," Trini said with a shriek.

"What in the heck are Were-Beasts?" Bulk whimpered.

"We come in many forms. Were-Lions! Were-Tigers! Were-Bears!" said Trini.

"Oh my," Skull whimpered.

"Please don't eat us," Bulk begged.

"I'll give you to the count of three to run away as fast as you can," Trini said. "1 . . . 2 . . ."

Bulk and Skull screamed again, and this time, the duo took off running into the night.

"And never come back, or we'll eat you," Trini shouted.

The scouts gathered together, laughing and exchanging high fives.

The fun then came to a screeching halt when Ms. Gertrude came stomping their way.

"What on earth are you all up to?" Ms. Gertrude barked.

"We were teaching those big jerks a lesson," Silvia said.

Ms. Gertrude scoffed and shot the scouts a look of disappointment. "Frightening people half to death is hardly what I would call a lesson. That is not proper Angel Scout behavior. I am deeply disappointed in all of you. That goes double for you, Ms. Kwan."

Trini took off her mask and slumped like a child who had just gotten in trouble with her parents. "Please don't be angry. We were just trying to have some fun."

"Fun and mischief all too often go hand in hand," Ms. Gertrude said, furiously writing notes on her clipboard. "Ms. Kwan, if you are going to be a scout leader, it will do you well to learn this. Now off to bed with all of you. We have a big day ahead of us tomorrow."

Hours later, Trini lay alone in her tent, tossing and turning in her sleeping bag. Far too many worrisome thoughts filled her mind for her to sleep. In the morning, she would be leading the scouts on a wilderness hike. With all the negative marks Ms. Gertrude had already given her, Trini wondered if it was still possible to pass the leadership exam.

Just when she began to nod off, her wrist-communicator chimed. She excitedly leaped upright. "What's up, Alpha 5?"

"I have good news and bad news," Alpha 5 said. "The good news is that I've located one of the four urns."

"That's great," Trini cheered. "So what's the bad news?"

"It's somewhere deep in the Australian Outback," Alpha 5 said.

Trini shrugged. "That doesn't sound too bad. I

can teleport there right now."

"You didn't let me finish," said Alpha 5. "Aye-yi-yi, the urn is stuck on the side of a rocky cliff over one hundred feet above the ground. If that isn't bad enough, it's being guarded by a giant scorpion. The mission will be perilous."

Chapter 10

The surface temperature of the Australian outback sweltered at over 120 degrees. The scorched ground cracked beneath Trini's feet when she teleported into the unforgiving wilderness. Alpha 5 had warned that the outback was one of the most dangerous environments on Earth. The region was inhabited by carnivorous beasts, birds of prey, and venomous reptiles.

Trini picked up a survival pack that Alpha 5 had sent ahead of her arrival. The cliff where the first urn resided was a few miles away. She would have teleported directly to the cliff, but Alpha 5 worried that the energy displacement created by a teleportation field could set off an avalanche.

It took Trini over an hour to hike across the hardened desert. Whenever she thought about stopping to rest, she reminded herself that she had to succeed or the other Rangers would remain trapped for all time. She also needed to get back to Angel Grove before the scouts awoke for breakfast.

A nervous twinge shot down Trini's spine as she approached the rocky cliff face. Jagged rocks and crumbling cracks lined every inch of its surface. Peering upward, Trini spotted a pink urn entangled in the roots of a long-dead tree poised over one hundred feet above the ground.

"Kimberly," Trini muttered. She then spoke into her communicator. "Alpha 5, I'm here. Though I don't see the scorpion you mentioned."

"Our sensors aren't picking up anything, either, but that doesn't mean it isn't still around," Alpha 5 replied.

Trini placed the backpack on the ground and opened the top flap. Inside she found a grappling hook launcher. She took aim at the cliff wall and pulled the trigger. The hook soared skyward, dragging a climbing cable along behind it. The hook jammed into the cliff wall a few yards above the pink urn.

Trini slipped on a pair of climbing gloves and gave the cable a firm pull. Assured that the cable was secure, she began to traverse her way up the treacherous surface. The trek upward was a slow and daunting process. Rocks cracked and chipped in her hands. The intense heat of the wind felt like fire blasting on her back.

It took Trini the better part of an hour to climb all the way up. Her hands trembled with fatigue as she reached back to lock the climbing cable to secure her position. With her hands free, she reached up for the pink urn. It took every bit of her concentration to avoid getting snagged on the thorny tree roots. When she finally got a grip on the urn, the thing wouldn't budge an inch. Even after ripping away some of the roots, she still couldn't pull it free.

"Alpha 5, the urn is jammed in tight," Trini said. "Do you have any ideas how I can get it loose?"

"I think I know what the problem is, and it's very bad," said Alpha 5.

Trini then saw what Alpha 5 was so worried about. The pink urn was locked in the pincer of a huge scorpion. The beast measured over twelve feet long and probably weighed hundreds of pounds. It took every bit of courage Trini had not to cry out in fear.

"Aye-yi-yi, Trini, you need to get out of there right away," said Alpha 5.

"Trini, this is Zordon; I'm afraid I have to agree

with Alpha 5. It's far too dangerous to face that beast on your own," he said.

"You're probably right, but I'm not leaving without that urn," Trini insisted. "The other Rangers wouldn't turn tail and run if I was trapped inside that thing."

"Understood. Do what you must and may the Power protect you," Zordon replied.

Trini climbed up another couple of feet so she could get a clear look at the scorpion. The best she could tell, the beast appeared to be sleeping. That was a huge relief. The thing was so big it could crush Trini's entire body in one of its massive pincers.

She reached out and gripped the pink urn firmly in both hands. Taking a deep breath, she pulled with all her might. The urn's smooth glossy surface made it tough to keep a grip. After a full minute of straining and pulling, the urn finally broke free.

"Got it," Trini exclaimed.

"Good work," Alpha 5 cheered. "Stand by, and I'll teleport you out of there."

The scorpion suddenly snapped awake and lurched forward. Trini couldn't move. She couldn't think. The only thing she could do was gasp in terror.

Chapter 11

Breathless and paralyzed by fear, Trini stared up at the scorpion. Before she could hope to react, the beast plucked the pink urn from her grip. It then reached out one of its massive pincers and snapped her climbing cable. Trini desperately gripped the cliff wall. The brittle rocks cracked and crumbled in her hands. At best, she had only seconds before she would plummet to her doom.

"Aye-yi-yi, Trini, you need to teleport out of there before it's too late," Alpha 5 yelped.

"I'm not going anywhere until I get that urn," Trini insisted.

Trini knew her only chance would be to morph into the Yellow Ranger, but with both her hands clinging to the cliff, that just wasn't an option. She first needed to get to a place stable enough so she could reach for her Morpher. Taking a quick look around, she spotted a small ledge a few yards to her left.

As Trini began to work her way across, she saw the scorpion staring down at her from above. Its red eyes glared so bright that she had to look away. The scorpion then let out a furious screech and stabbed at Trini with its venomous tail. The strike missed her by mere inches, and the scorpion's tail bashed into the cliff. Sharp rocks scattered toward Trini, scratching up her arm and leg.

Trini reached out for the ledge desperately, but it was just beyond her reach. With no other choice, she found two solid footholds, crouched down low, and took a deep breath. Then, with every bit of strength she could muster, she made a daring leap for the ledge. Her valiant effort proved to be just enough to make it all the way. She caught the edge and quickly scurried the rest of the way up.

Glancing back, Trini saw the scorpion crawling along the cliff wall, jamming its pincers into the rocks as it moved. At the speed the beast was coming, it would reach her in only seconds. With no time to catch her breath, Trini grabbed her Morpher and extended her arms.

"It's Morphin Time!" she shouted.

Now morphed into the Yellow Ranger, Trini set

her sights on taking the urn back from the scorpion. Without hesitation, she lunged at the menacing creature. The scorpion tried to smack the Yellow Ranger away with its pincer, but she twisted around and dodged the strike. With one hand, she grabbed on to the scorpion's massive head. With the other hand, she punched the beast right between the eyes. The strike caused the scorpion to stumble.

With the beast knocked out of its senses, the Yellow Ranger grabbed the pink urn and tucked it under one arm. She gripped the cliff with her free hand and looked into the scorpion's eyes. "This is the part where you go tumbling down."

The Yellow Ranger raised a leg high and then kicked downward with all her might. The walloping strike caused the scorpion to lose its grip on the wall. Its legs flailed helplessly as it plummeted and crashed onto the rocky ground below.

The Yellow Ranger gasped rapidly to catch her breath. She tapped her communicator to teleport away, but just as at the museum, a yellow energy field flickered around her and then faded away. She tried again, with the same result. "Alpha 5, can you hear me?"

"I read you loud and clear, Trini," Alpha 5 replied.

"I'm having trouble teleporting again," the Yellow Ranger replied. "Any chance you can get me out of here?"

"Right away," Alpha 5 said. "And if I may say so, you were awesome."

Chapter 12

At the Command Center, Alpha 5 waved a digital scanning wand over the pink urn. Trini hunched in exhaustion, still gasping to catch her breath. There were several scrapes and scratches on her arms and legs, but she had more important concerns at the moment.

"Alpha 5, please tell me you can get Kimberly out of that thing," Trini said.

"Aye-yi-yi," Alpha 5 said. "I'm afraid the urn is sealed by nanotronic energy."

"Well, now we at least know the source of the nanotronic energy," Trini said, then looked up at Zordon. "Do you think that being near the urns is what's causing my communicator to malfunction when I try to use it to teleport?"

Zordon nodded. "That is a certainty. It also means that whenever you are near any of the urns, you won't be able to teleport on your own. We will have to rely on the systems here at the Command Center."

Alpha 5 stepped up next to Trini. "And to make it even worse, until we figure out how to defuse the nanotronic energy, we won't be able to free the Rangers from the urns," he yelped.

"Then we'll smash the urn to bits," Trini insisted. "We must have something around here that can bust through this thing."

Zordon looked at Trini. "I'm sorry, but we have no way of knowing what effect that would have on Kimberly. Our only choice is to find a way to dispel the mystical seal."

"So then I've failed the Rangers again," Trini lamented.

"That is not true," Zordon said. "If not for your bravery, we would have never recovered the urn. You've taken us one step closer to saving the other Rangers."

Trini shrugged in half-hearted agreement. "I won't rest until we recover all four urns and all my friends are finally free."

"We won't rest, either. Not for a second. Or even a nanosecond," said Alpha 5.

Trini smiled warmly. "Thank you, both of you."

"Then it is settled. We will continue working here, and you shall return to Angel Grove. I believe you have a hike to lead today," Zordon said.

"Oh no! I nearly forgot," Trini said, checking her watch. "I just hope I can still make it in time."

On the observation deck of the Moon Palace, the Griffin Pharaoh was still sitting on Rita's throne. Putty Patrollers fanned him with large palm leaves, while others served him grapes from a golden bowl.

Squatt and Baboo raced in the door, tripping and stumbling in a frantic frenzy.

"Griffin Pharaoh, this has gone on long enough," Squatt yelped. "The Yellow Ranger just found one of the urns, and you need to do something about it."

The Griffin Pharaoh laughed deviously. "I don't care if that inferior Yellow Ranger finds all four urns. Only I, the great Griffin Pharaoh, know how to open them. Now get out of my sight."

Baboo puffed up his chest, trying to look tough. "I think you're a little mixed up about who's in charge around here."

Squatt folded his arms, also trying to look tough.

"Now get off your golden butt this minute, or we'll—"

The Griffin Pharaoh leaped to his feet. He bashed Squatt and Baboo with his cyclone staff, hard enough to knock them to the floor. "Take this as my final warning, peasant fools. Question my authority one more time, and I'll blast you both clear across the cosmos," he shouted.

Finster, who had been watching quietly from the corner, decided it was time to step in. "Greetings, Griffin Pharaoh. May I most humbly approach your greatness?"

The Griffin Pharaoh pointed his staff at Finster. "Who are you, and what is your purpose?"

Finster bowed nervously. "I am here to serve you, great Griffin Pharaoh. And, if I may be so humble, to offer you a bit of valuable advice."

The Griffin Pharaoh glared at Finster. "You may speak, but you had better speak well."

Finster moved closer. "It's about the Power Ranger that escaped from your clutches. It would be in your best interest to return to Earth and capture her as soon as possible."

"If you're speaking of that yellow coward, she is of no concern to me," the Griffin Pharaoh said.

"I must humbly disagree," said Finster. "Our Queen Rita battled these Power Rangers many times. They are quite cunning. Disregarding even one of them could be a disastrous mistake."

The Griffin Pharaoh considered this carefully and nodded. "Very well. In that case, I will deal with this Yellow Ranger."

"A wise decision, your greatness," Finster said, breathing a sigh of relief.

The Griffin Pharaoh looked at Squatt and Baboo. "Seek out the Yellow Ranger and tell her that I, the great Griffin Pharaoh, have decreed that on this day, we shall meet on the field of battle." He then waved his staff and the fifth urn magically appeared before him. "When she arrives, I will trap her in my final urn, and these meddlesome Power Rangers will trouble me no longer."

Squatt approached the Griffin Pharaoh nervously. "And how do we get her to agree to face you?" the dimwitted sidekick said. "The Yellow Ranger will know it's a trap."

Finster nodded. "We will need some sort of bait to lure her out."

The Griffin Pharaoh thought for a moment. "Tell

the Yellow Ranger that I will bring an urn containing one of her Ranger friends. If she can defeat me in battle, then it shall be her prize."

"And we'll be there to make sure that she loses," Finster muttered wickedly.

Chapter 13

Trini teleported directly into her tent at the Angel Grove Campground. After a night of battling the giant scorpion in the blistering heat, she felt exhausted and much in need of some sleep. Rest would have to come later, she told herself, and then made a quick change into her Angel Scout hiking outfit.

Moments later, Trini hurried out of her tent and was disheartened to find that the scouts were already gone. Ms. Gertrude must have grown tired of waiting for her and decided to lead the hike herself.

For the next half hour, Trini raced along the hiking path. She searched every place the scouts would have gone. They weren't at the bird sanctuary, or the wildlife refuge, or the wading pond. By the time Trini reached the upper ridge, she'd begun to worry. As much as she hated interrupting Alpha 5 and Zordon's search for the other Rangers, she needed to know that the scouts weren't in danger.

"Alpha 5, do you read me?" Trini said into her communicator.

"Alpha 5 here," he replied. "If you're calling for an update on the search, unfortunately I have nothing new to report."

"Sorry to hear that," said Trini with a disappointed sigh. "But I'm actually calling to see if you could do a scan of the hiking trail. I'm trying to locate the scouts."

"Just give me one minute to align the scanners," Alpha 5 said.

Trini waited nervously as Alpha 5 performed the search. She would never forgive herself if something bad had happened to the scouts.

After a few tense moments, Alpha 5 finally replied, "Aye-yi-yi, I've found the scouts. They're hiding out in the ancient painted caves."

"Hiding from what?" Trini asked urgently.

"Not from what! From whom," Alpha 5 yelped. "Squatt and Baboo are outside the cave with a squad of Putty Patrollers."

"Copy, Alpha 5, I'm on my way," she said and then pulled out her Morpher. "It's Morphin Time!"

Trini morphed into the Yellow Ranger and teleported directly into the painted caves. The rocky walls were decorated with images created by a tribe that had lived in Angel Grove thousands of years ago. During a search of the expansive caverns, the Yellow Ranger found Ms. Gertrude, Silvia, and the other scouts huddled behind a rock formation. All the girls lit up with excitement when they saw the Yellow Ranger.

"I told you the Power Rangers would save us," Silvia said in amazement.

Ms. Gertrude was equally awestruck. "Thank you for coming, Ms. Yellow Ranger. How did you find us?"

"You can thank Trini Kwan. She's been searching for you," the Yellow Ranger said.

"But how did Trini know?" Silvia asked.

"No time to explain," the Yellow Ranger said. "I'm going out there to deal with the monsters. I want you all to wait just inside the cave entrance. When I give the signal, make a break for the hiking path and head straight back to your camp as fast as you can."

Ms. Gertrude and the scouts all nodded.

The Yellow Ranger led the scouts toward the cave's main entrance. The scouts took cover behind a large boulder. When the Yellow Ranger stepped out of the cave, a dozen Putty Patrollers raced over and circled around her.

Squatt and Baboo were standing at the far end of the rocky area outside the cave.

"We were wondering when you would show up, Yellow Ranger," said Squatt.

"And just so you know, we know you're hiding those scouts inside the cave," said Baboo.

The Yellow Ranger raised a fist. "And just so you know, if you do anything to hurt those scouts, you'll have my fist to answer to."

"Cool your jets," Squatt said. "We're just here to deliver a message."

"The Griffin Pharaoh wants to fight you," said Baboo. "He says you have to meet him at the rock quarry in one hour."

The Yellow Ranger shook her head. "I'm not letting him trap me in one of his urns. Tell him I'm not falling for his tricks."

"It's no trick. It's a challenge," Squatt said. "The Griffin Pharaoh says if you can beat him, your prize will be an urn that one of your Ranger friends is trapped in."

"And just in case you're not getting it, you can either go fight him there, or you can fight us here," Baboo said.

The Yellow Ranger now understood what Squatt and Baboo were up to. If she refused to meet the Griffin Pharaoh at the rock quarry, the scouts would be in great danger.

"Fine. If you let the scouts go free, I'll fight the Griffin Pharaoh," the Yellow Ranger said.

"Then we have a deal," said Squatt.

"Come out, come out, little scouts," Baboo shouted.

Ms. Gertrude and the scouts peered out from the cave.

"It's okay," said the Yellow Ranger. "Head back to camp, and don't stop for anything."

Ms. Gertrude and the scouts nervously emerged from the cave and hurried toward the hiking path. They soon were heading off down the trail to safety.

"We've kept our part of the deal," said Squatt. "Now you'd better keep your part, or your precious scouts won't be so lucky next time."

Chapter 14

Trini stood looking at the Command Center's viewing globe. It displayed an aerial view of a rock quarry located on the outskirts of Angel Grove. Machines were busy ripping deep into the earth, forming a rocky canyon fifty feet deep and over a mile wide.

"Aye-yi-yi," Alpha 5 yelped, pacing in a frantic frenzy. "This is a terrible idea. Zordon, please try to talk some sense into her."

"I'm sorry, Alpha 5, but Squatt and Baboo have left us with no choice," Zordon said.

"I already gave my word that I would go. It was the only way I could assure the safety of the scouts," Trini said.

"But you'll be walking right into a trap," Alpha 5 said.

"Alpha 5 is correct," Zordon said. "There is no doubt that the Griffin Pharaoh will attempt to trap you in the fifth urn. If that were to happen, you and the other Rangers could remain captive for all time."

Trini nodded nervously. "It could also be a chance to get one of the missing urns. I have to try."

Zordon carefully considered this. "Very well. Remember, the Griffin Pharaoh's nanotronic energy may prevent you from using your communicator to teleport."

Trini understood. "Then I'm going to have to rely on you and Alpha 5 to do that for me. Actually, my entire plan depends on it."

Alpha 5 stood straight and saluted Trini. "You can count on us. We won't let you down."

"Then it's decided," Trini said, holding out her Morpher. "Back to action!"

The Yellow Ranger teleported to the upper rim of the rock quarry. The pit looked far more treacherous than it had when she saw it on the viewing globe. Her heart began to race as she cautiously made her way down a steep embankment. With every step forward, she had to be careful not to slip on the loose chunks of gravel scattered all over the ground.

"Alpha 5, I don't see any sign of Squatt and Baboo. What about you?" the Yellow Ranger asked.

"Nothing yet, but there are so many places those

two could be hiding," said Alpha 5.

The Yellow Ranger then heard a thunderous rumbling that sounded like thousands of rolling rocks. She turned around and saw an avalanche of gravel was pouring down the embankment, seconds from crushing her. With no other place to go, the Yellow Ranger frantically raced farther down into the quarry. All along the way, she nearly tumbled off her feet as she slipped and slid on the loose gravel covering every inch of the ground.

"Aye-yi-yi, Trini, I'm going to teleport you to a safe place," Alpha 5 cried.

"If you do that, it will ruin my whole plan," the Yellow Ranger replied.

After dashing along for another hundred yards, the Yellow Ranger finally reached the bottom of the embankment. She made a diving leap to the side, just in time to avoid being buried under the wave of rocks.

"That was much too close," Alpha 5 yelped. "You could have been buried alive."

A chill shot down the Yellow Ranger's spine when she saw just how right Alpha 5 was. "Well, it didn't happen, so we proceed with the plan."

The Yellow Ranger heard the sound of heavy feet

trekking through gravel. She made a quick turn and saw Squatt walking her way. The blubbering brute was clutching the blue urn in his arms.

"Billy," the Yellow Ranger whispered.

"I almost thought you weren't going to make it, Yellow Ranger," said Squatt.

The Yellow Ranger took a fighting stance. "Where is the Griffin Pharaoh?"

From another direction, the Yellow Ranger heard footsteps. She turned and saw Baboo was approaching.

"Don't you worry. The Griffin Pharaoh will be here any minute now," said Baboo. "But before he arrives, let's have some fun."

In a white flash, a squad of Putty Patrollers appeared. They began to circle the Yellow Ranger. She took a quick look around and counted at least twelve of the clay brutes.

"You must be joking," the Yellow Ranger said. "I could take down this many Putties in my sleep."

"Oh yeah, then let's see if we can find some more for you to fight," said Squatt.

Putty Patrollers dashed out from behind the construction machines and gravel mounds. The

Yellow Ranger gasped as they began to swarm her. She looked around again, only this time there were too many to count or, more importantly, far more than she could possibly fight on her own.

The Yellow Ranger sighed. "I just had to go and open my big mouth."

Chapter 15

"Trini, just say the word and I'll teleport you back to the Command Center," Alpha 5 cried from her communicator.

The Yellow Ranger could hardly hear Alpha 5 over the sound of her heart thumping in her chest. In every direction she looked, all she could see were Putty Patrollers; more than she had ever faced in a single battle.

Squatt shook a fist at the Putty Patrollers. "What are you fools waiting for? Capture the Yellow Ranger."

All at once, the gray-skinned brutes charged at the Yellow Ranger. She counterattacked with a barrage of dazzling punches and kicks. The first wave of Putty Patrollers went down in quick order. The next wave to attack proved to be a lot tougher. They clutched at her arms and legs. Gripped her around the waist. Kicked her legs out from under her and shoved her down.

Soon, the Yellow Ranger was on her knees, fully

restrained and unable to break free.

"Aye-yi-yi, this has gone far enough," Alpha 5 yelped. "I'm getting you out of there right now."

Zordon then spoke on the communicator. "I have to agree with Alpha 5. The situation has become far too dangerous."

"Not yet! We have to wait for the perfect moment, or this will have all been for nothing," the Yellow Ranger insisted.

"Step aside, you worthless peasants," the voice of the Griffin Pharaoh bellowed from deep within the horde of Putty Patrollers. The gray-skinned thugs scattered to make a path for the winged beast. The Griffin Pharaoh stopped a few yards short of the Yellow Ranger.

Squatt raced over and placed the blue urn right next to the Griffin Pharaoh.

The Griffin Pharaoh stared at the Yellow Ranger. "So you're the one they're all making a big fuss over. You don't look so tough to me."

"Tell these thugs to let me go, and I'll show you how tough I am," the Yellow Ranger said.

"A waste of time. You could never hope to defeat me," the Griffin Pharaoh said. With a wave of his staff, the fifth urn appeared with the top hinged open. Just as in the museum, a shadow-hand arose from inside. The Yellow Ranger's eyes went wide with fear as the abomination floated her way.

The Putty Patrollers restraining the Yellow Ranger began to tremble.

"Aye-yi-yi, Trini, please tell me it's time," Alpha 5 yelped.

"Just a few more seconds," the Yellow Ranger said, taking a deep breath. She waited until the shadow-hand was only inches away from her. "Now!"

In a flash, Alpha 5 teleported her away. Then an instant later, she appeared next to the Griffin Pharaoh. "I'll be taking my prize," she said.

"Treacherous peasant, I will crush you," the Griffin Pharaoh roared.

"Not today, you won't," the Yellow Ranger said. She executed a lightning-quick barrage of spin kicks, hitting the Griffin Pharaoh in the jaw again and again. The strikes caused thousands of pieces of the Griffin Pharaoh's Nanosand to scatter like dust in the wind, and his jaw turned back to lifeless stone.

"You can't hurt me. I am invincible," the Griffin Pharaoh roared. The scattered Nanosand swarmed back to his face and transformed his jaw back into living flesh.

"Zordon, did you see that?" Trini asked, gasping fearfully.

"I did, and I believe it is time for you to get out of there," Zordon replied.

"You don't have to tell me twice," the Yellow Ranger said, then made a dive roll across the ground and popped up next to the blue urn.

"Stop her, you fools," the Griffin Pharaoh shouted to the Putty Patrollers.

The Putty Patrollers scurried toward the Yellow Ranger.

"Too slow," the Yellow Ranger said, grabbing the blue urn and teleporting away.

"Curse you, Yellow Ranger! I will have my revenge," the Griffin Pharaoh roared.

Chapter 16

Following her battle with the Griffin Pharaoh, Trini returned to the Command Center. Alpha 5 and Zordon got right to work on their analysis of the blue urn. As much as Trini wanted to stay and help, Zordon felt it was best for her to return to the Angel Grove Campground to ensure the scouts were safe.

Upon her arrival, she found that they had already packed up and returned to the city. She felt relieved that the scouts were out of harm's way, but was also disappointed that she had missed her chance to lead them on the hike.

Her stomach grumbling with hunger, Trini decided to go to the Youth Center to get a bite to eat. As she scarfed down a veggie sandwich and an extra-large berry smoothie, she looked at the empty chairs around the table. She couldn't recall ever feeling as alone as she did in that moment.

Ernie approached carrying a tray with a large

ice cream sundae. "I don't mean to nose into your business, but are you okay?"

Trini shrugged half-heartedly. "I'm just having a really tough day."

"I'm betting it has to do with what happened up at the campground," Ernie said. "It's a good thing that Power Ranger showed up when she did, or who knows what might have happened."

Trini looked up at Ernie, a little surprised. "News sure travels fast around here."

"Even faster when the Power Rangers are involved," Ernie said with a gleaming smile. "I don't know who they are, but I do know they're about the bravest bunch of heroes who have ever lived."

Trini cracked a little smile. "You really think so?"

Ernie nodded an affirmative. "I know so. Everyone in Angel Grove would back me up on that. I hope those Rangers know how grateful we are for everything they do for us."

Trini smiled a little brighter. This was exactly what she had needed to hear. "I have a feeling they do know. And you even helped me feel better about something. Thank you, Ernie."

"Don't exactly know what I did, but I'm sure glad

I could help," Ernie said with a proud grin. "Anyway, I need to deliver this ice cream sundae before it melts and I catch all heck from Ms. Gertrude."

"You mean she's here?" Trini looked back and saw Ms. Gertrude sitting at a table on the far end of the room. As usual, she was writing notes on her clipboard. "Ernie, would you mind if I delivered that sundae?"

Ernie shrugged. "Don't see why not. And if you ever want a job waiting tables, you just let old Ernie know." He handed the serving tray to Trini and strutted away.

Trini took a deep breath and began to walk over to Ms. Gertrude. In her mind, Trini could already hear Ms. Gertrude telling her that she failed the leadership exam and then proceeding to list every single thing she had done wrong.

Trini cleared her throat. "Excuse me, Ms. Gertrude. I have your sundae."

Ms. Gertrude looked up, surprised to see Trini. "Ms. Kwan, I didn't know you were employed here."

Trini put the sundae on the table in front of Ms. Gertrude. "Actually, I'm not. I was just hoping we could talk about what happened at the campground."

"Honestly, my nerves are still a bit too shaken to

discuss that," Ms. Gertrude said. She took a heaping bite of the sundae and smiled with delight. She then gestured for Trini to sit down. "I bet you think I'm a terrible old ogre who just wants to put down everything you do."

Trini looked away, unable to entirely disagree. "I wouldn't call you an ogre."

"It wouldn't be an unfair assessment," Ms. Gertrude admitted. "And speaking of terrible ogres, did I ever tell you about the scout leader I had when I was a kid?"

Trini shook her head.

Ms. Gertrude took another bite of her sundae. "Her name was Ms. Vivian. She was a dreadful scout leader. She was always tardy for meetings, if she bothered to show up at all. The woman loathed camping and hiking and just about anything that required her to go outdoors."

"Then why would she want to be an Angel Scout leader?" Trini asked.

"Your guess is as good as mine," Ms. Gertrude said with a frown. "All I ever wanted was to be the best Angel Scout I could be, and she made that downright impossible."

Trini looked at Ms. Gertrude's sash, covered in merit badges. "How can that be? You're one of the most successful Angel Scouts to ever wear the uniform."

Ms. Gertrude smiled proudly. "That is true, but most of those merits were earned during my time as a leader, not when I was a scout."

"I'm so sorry to hear that," Trini said warmly.

"Don't feel too bad for me," Ms. Gertrude said, sitting up straight. "The experience taught me the importance of strong leadership, so when my time came to become a scout leader, I vowed to be the best leader I could be. I also vowed to only allow those who are equally committed to become scout leaders."

Trini considered this and realized why Ms. Gertrude had been so hard on her. "You want to make sure that no scout ever has to have a bad experience like you did."

Ms. Gertrude looked Trini right in the eyes. "So I ask you, Trini Kwan: What kind of leader would you be, when and if you manage to pass your exam?"

Trini eyed Ms. Gertrude curiously. "Are you saying that I haven't already failed?"

"Do you believe you have failed?" Ms. Gertrude asked.

"No, I don't," Trini said firmly. "And I won't make excuses about things that have gone wrong, but I would like a chance to prove to you that I can do things right."

"And how do you intend to do that?" Ms. Gertrude asked.

Trini was quick to make a plan. "The playground at Angel Grove Park was recently damaged by some of those creatures we saw at the campground. I want to lead a Community Fix Up to repair the damage."

"That's an admirable plan. And when would this happen?" Ms. Gertrude asked.

"Tomorrow at eight in the morning," Trini said.

Ms. Gertrude wrote a note on her clipboard. "Then you'd better move quickly, because that gives you precious little time to pull it all together."

"I won't let you down again," Trini promised. Just then, her communicator chimed. Alpha 5 was calling her from the Command Center. "And it looks like I need to get going. Thank you again, Ms. Gertrude."

Chapter 17

Trini's communicator chimed again as she raced out the front door of the Youth Center.

"Alpha 5, please say you have some good news for me," Trini said.

"You bet I do. Our analysis of the blue and pink urns have helped us to narrow our search parameters for the other two," Alpha 5 said.

"And?" Trini awaited eagerly.

"And we've already found the approximate location of one of the urns," said Alpha 5.

"Why is the location only approximate?" Trini asked.

"Because it's in an underground cavern made entirely of ice, and it's located in . . ." Alpha 5 paused nervously. "Antarctica!"

Trini shrugged. "Doesn't sound any more dangerous than fighting a giant scorpion on the side of a cliff."

"Trini, this is Zordon," he announced on the communicator. "Do not take the danger of this mission lightly. In addition to the subzero temperatures, the urn is guarded by a serpopard: a vicious sea serpent and leopard hybrid monster with a murderous temperament."

As frightening as that all sounded, Trini wasn't about to allow a dangerous beast to stop her from saving her friends. "Understood, Zordon. Now please teleport me to the closest point possible."

"As you wish. And may the Power protect you," Zordon replied.

Trini looked around to make sure nobody was watching and then morphed into the Yellow Ranger. She teleported thousands of miles across the world, arriving on the middle of a glacier in the frozen land of Antarctica. Her Ranger suit did well to protect her from the subzero weather, though she could still feel the chill of the freezing wind on the back of her neck.

For a moment, she stood, taking in the astounding beauty of the Antarctic landscape. Looking toward the north, she saw ice and snow that went on for as far as the eye could see. And to the south, she marveled at the sight of ice cliffs towering hundreds of feet high.

"Trini, I don't mean to rush you," Alpha 5 said, "but we've detected a storm heading in your direction. You need to complete the mission as quickly as possible."

The Yellow Ranger began a tedious trek across the ice. She passed a colony of penguins marching in formation. With each passing minute, the sky rapidly darkened. Black storm clouds would soon cover the twilight sun.

Traversing down a slippery ridge, the Yellow Ranger reached the entrance to the cavern. The jagged icy archway towered over one hundred feet high and fifty feet across. Beyond the entrance, there was nothing to be seen but a stark void of darkness.

"It looks a lot creepier than I could have imagined," the Yellow Ranger said.

"Aye-yi-yi, Trini, you really don't have to do this," Alpha 5 replied.

Trini took a calming breath and pushed her fears aside. "I could never live with myself if I quit now."

The Yellow Ranger walked through the archway and headed into the darkness of the ice cavern. High above, she saw razor-sharp shards of ice covering every inch of the ceiling. The walls creaked and crackled, as if the cavern could come crashing down at any second.

"Alpha 5, any word on how stable this cavern is?" the Yellow Ranger whispered.

There was no response.

"Alpha 5! Zordon! Please respond," the Yellow Ranger said urgently.

Again, there was no response. The thick cavern walls were blocking the signal. From this point on, the Yellow Ranger would be on her own. Just then, she heard feet shuffling along the icy floor, not far behind her. She stood perfectly still for a tense moment, not daring to take a breath. Judging by the pattern of the footsteps, she guessed that whatever was coming her way had more than two legs.

"I sure hope that's not the serpopard," she whispered.

Hurrying deeper into the cavern, the Yellow Ranger slipped and slid on the icy floor. The tunnel became narrower and narrower, forcing her to turn sideways to continue. She hoped a creature as large as a serpopard would be unable to follow in such cramped corridors. This hope was quashed when she heard the thunderous sounds of the creature smashing its way through the ice.

With her heart racing, the Yellow Ranger squeezed through a small opening at the end of the tunnel. When she emerged on the other side, she realized she was standing atop a steep embankment. Her feet slipped out from beneath her, and she went sliding downward on her back.

The Yellow Ranger tried to grab on to the cavern wall. There was no place to get a grip. She jammed her boots into the ground. It was much too slippery to catch traction. She tried everything she could think of to slow her descent, but nothing made a bit of difference.

Just when it seemed the situation couldn't get worse, the Yellow Ranger soared off the edge of a cliff and began to plummet into a pit of absolute darkness.

Chapter 18

"Zordon! Alpha 5! If you can hear me, I don't think I'm going to make it," the Yellow Ranger shouted into her communicator. She was helplessly plummeting deeper and deeper into the dark abyss. Making it all the worse, she could hear the serpopard roaring from up above. She wasn't sure if the beast had slipped off the cliff or maliciously jumped after her. Either way, she just hoped the thing wouldn't crash down on top of her when they hit the ground.

SLAM!

Without a bit of warning, the Yellow Ranger crashed into the icy cavern floor. The thud of the impact thundered in her head. The air was forced from her lungs. She felt dizzy, as if the world was spinning around her. She couldn't think. She couldn't move. She couldn't breathe.

The Yellow Ranger snapped back to her senses when she heard the thundering thump of the serpopard slamming into the ground somewhere nearby. As she gasped to catch her breath, she also heard the labored breathing of the serpopard. Somehow they had both managed to survive their harrowing falls.

The Yellow Ranger knew she needed to get moving quickly. It took every bit of will she had to get to her feet. Just then, a pair of flaming red eyes, each the size of her head, peered at her. The Yellow Ranger yelped in terror. The beast wasn't just alive; it was on its feet and ready for a fight.

The glossy gray-skinned serpopard towered over fifteen feet from head to tail. It stood on four legs and had a body that resembled a leopard. The head of a sea serpent stared down from atop a lanky neck.

The Yellow Ranger raised her fists for a fight. "I came here for the urn, and I'm not leaving without it."

The serpopard replied with a thunderous roar. Two searing beams of fire then blasted out from its massive eyes. The Yellow Ranger made a desperate leap to the side, barely evading the attack. She looked over and saw a hole, burned into the icy floor, that spanned several feet wide.

The Yellow Ranger reached into her side holster

and pulled out her blade blaster. She took quick aim and squeezed off several energy bolts. The serpopard roared as the shots burned a hole in its torso. Seconds later, the flesh began to rapidly rejuvenate over the damaged area. Just before it completely healed over, the Yellow Ranger saw something inside the serpopard that resembled a black urn.

Refusing to give up, the Yellow Ranger continued firing as fast as she could, scoring several more hits. The serpopard slowed as the shots burned another hole in its side. Before the flesh could heal over, the Yellow Ranger flipped high into the air and landed on the creature's back.

She looked into the hole and was astonished to see the serpopard was hollow. The beast didn't have any organs, or bones, nor a single drop of blood. The only thing the Yellow Ranger did see was the black urn rolling around inside its torso.

"Zack," the Yellow Ranger said. She tried to reach inside for the black urn, but the serpopard bucked around, sending her soaring away.

"You're not getting rid of me that easily," the Yellow Ranger shouted. She raised her hands high, and a pair of short-bladed Power Daggers appeared in them. "Now we finish this."

The serpopard roared and fired several searing blasts from its eyes. The Yellow Ranger leaped, rolled, and flipped clear of every shot. She looked back and saw a dozen holes burned into the icy walls. The floor began to shake with a thundering rumble. The walls began to crack and crumble. The cavern was moments from caving in.

The serpopard knew what was happening and began to back away, but the Yellow Ranger wasn't about to let the beast get away now. Gritting her teeth, she raised the Power Daggers and charged forward. She spiraled high into the air and again landed on the serpopard's back. The beast bucked furiously, trying to knock her off. This time, the Yellow Ranger was ready. She jammed one of the Power Daggers into the serpopard's back and held on tight.

The Yellow Ranger used her other Power Dagger to hack a hole in the serpopard's torso, exposing the black urn. She then dropped the dagger and reached inside the serpopard. The beast bucked again, this time even harder than before. The Yellow Ranger grabbed the black urn a mere heartbeat before being thrown off the serpopard's back.

The instant the Yellow Ranger's feet hit the ground, she broke into a desperate sprint. Falling chunks of ice pelted her helmet. The cavern ceiling was caving in quickly. She had to get out of the cave before being buried alive.

For the next several minutes, the Yellow Ranger ran through the endless tunnels with the urn gripped tight in her arms. She didn't need to look back to know the serpopard was in pursuit and trying to blast her with beams of fire. Again and again the shots narrowly missed, instead hitting the cavern walls and ceiling.

Just when it seemed she would never escape, the Yellow Ranger found the cavern's main entrance. It was about a hundred yards ahead of her, and just beyond it, there was sunlight.

"Alpha 5, if you can hear me, I could really use some help," the Yellow Ranger shouted.

"You don't know the half of it," Alpha 5 replied. "The cavern entrance is about to—"

Before Alpha 5 could finish, the archway entrance started to collapse. Thousands of razor-sharp shards of ice plummeted downward. The serpopard roared furiously as shard after shard impaled its body. The

Yellow Ranger dodged and weaved around the falling shards, just avoiding getting ripped to pieces.

"Alpha 5, now would be a really good time," the Yellow Ranger shouted.

"Aye-yi-yi! Just hold on a few more seconds," Alpha 5 replied.

Just then, the entire ceiling collapsed. The Yellow Ranger screamed in terror, certain it was the end.

"Engaging teleportation now," Alpha 5 cried out.

A mere instant before the Yellow Ranger would have been crushed, Alpha 5 teleported her away to safety.

Chapter 19

In the Moon Palace, several Putty Patrollers huddled fearfully in the corner. They were trying to stay clear of Squatt and Baboo, who were thrashing and bashing around in a furious frenzy.

"The Yellow Ranger has now found three of the four urns," Baboo ranted.

"This is all your fault, Baboo. I should never have let you talk me into going along with this moronic plan," said Squatt.

Squatt and Baboo wrestled like a pair of squabbling children.

Finster entered carrying a jeweled crown with flickering lights and glowing cables sticking out from the sides. "What foolishness are you two up to now?"

Squatt and Baboo stopped wrestling and glared at Finster.

"This foolishness is all your fault," Squatt said.

"You're absolutely right, Squatt. We shouldn't

be fighting each other when Finster is obviously to blame," Baboo said.

"If you two stop yapping for a minute, I could tell you that I've created a solution for our problem with the Griffin Pharaoh," Finster said, holding up the crown. "This crown, once placed atop his head, will render him under our complete control."

Squatt and Baboo glared at the flimsily constructed crown.

"How do you plan to get that crown onto his head?" Squatt asked.

"After the battle at the rock quarry, he took off, and we haven't seen him since," Squatt said.

"Then I suggest you two stop horsing around and start looking for him," Finster said. "We have to get this mess under control before Rita returns, or else."

"Or else what?" Squatt and Baboo asked.

Finster trembled, not wanting to even think about what Rita would do to them.

After delivering the black urn to Alpha 5, Trini headed to the Youth Center to meet up with the Angel Scouts. Upon her arrival, she was surprised to find the scouts were busy signing up volunteers for the Community Fix Up. Ms. Gertrude oversaw the effort attentively and, as always, she wrote plenty of notes on her clipboard.

Silvia dashed over gleefully and hugged Trini. "I'm so happy you finally made it."

"Sorry I'm late again. I was helping out some friends who got themselves in a major jam," Trini said. She looked over and met the disapproving glare of Ms. Gertrude.

"Don't let her get to you," Silvia whispered. "We've already signed up almost fifty volunteers for the Fix Up on Saturday, but I think we can get a hundred."

Trini smiled graciously. "You're all doing such amazing work. Thank you so much!"

"Oh, I have something cool to show you," Silvia said, taking Trini by the hand and leading her over to a table. She opened her backpack and took out a large book with the title *Myths and Legends of Ancient Egypt.* "There's an entire chapter in here about that Griffin Pharaoh guy we saw at the museum."

"That's great," Trini said. "I'm so happy you're taking the Historical Research Merit Badge project so seriously."

"I don't care about a dumb merit badge," Silvia said, flipping through the pages of the book. "I just want to show Daisy that I'm right about how the Power Rangers defeated the Griffin Pharaoh." She glared at Daisy on the other side of the room. Daisy looked over and stuck out her tongue. Silvia did the same.

Trini sighed. "It's not good to focus your energy on just trying to prove people wrong. Angel Scouts are about friendship and unity."

"If being an Angel Scout means having to be friends with Daisy, then count me out," Silvia said, crossing her arms in refusal. "I could never be friends with a stuck-up cheerleader."

Trini held Silvia's hand. "You should never judge people until you get to know them. My best friend, Kimberly, is a cheerleader. My friend Billy is a science whiz. Zack is an amazing dancer. And Jason is one of the best martial artists I've ever known. They're all into totally different things, but we're all great friends just the same."

Silvia shrugged, not entirely convinced. "I guess I never thought of it that way. Maybe I'll give Daisy a chance, but no promises."

"That's a great start," Trini said proudly. She then

noticed that Ms. Gertrude, standing nearby, had been listening in the whole time. Ms. Gertrude wrote a note on her clipboard and walked away. Trini sighed and then turned her attention back to Silvia. "So tell me what you've learned about the infamous Griffin Pharaoh."

Silvia turned to a page she had bookmarked. "At the museum, we learned about how the Griffin Pharaoh trapped all his enemies in magic urns, and then he used his powers to hypnotize everyone into being his mindless servants. What we didn't learn is that he made everyone build him a giant pyramid in the middle of the city and ruled over them like a big jerk for ninety-nine years."

"That's a really long time," Trini said. "Did you ever figure out how he was defeated?"

Silvia pointed to a drawing of the Griffin Pharaoh. He was refusing to fight a long line of warriors. "A lot of great warriors challenged him, but he would never accept a fight because he said he would only fight those who were worthy. I think he just used that as an excuse because he was afraid to lose. But someone must have defeated him."

Trini's communicator chimed. She let out a long

sigh. Of all the times Alpha 5 could be calling, this was the worst possible moment. If she were to walk away now, Ms. Gertrude would think she was flaking out again.

"What's that beeping sound?" Silvia asked.

For a moment, Trini debated if she should answer right away, or if it could wait just a little longer. Before she could decide either way, the communicator chimed again. It had to be urgent or Alpha 5 would not have been so persistent.

"I'm sorry, Silvia, I have to go," Trini said, then raced for the exit.

"Wait. Not already," Silvia said, slumping in disappointment.

Chapter 20

Trini's communicator chimed again as she exited the Youth Center.

"Alpha 5, please tell me you're calling about the last missing urn," Trini said into her communicator.

"I am, Trini, and the situation is desperately urgent. Somehow the urn ended up in a Dumpster in Tokyo," said Alpha 5.

"That doesn't sound so bad. I've always wanted to visit Japan," Trini said.

"The *where* isn't the problem," Alpha 5 replied. "The Dumpster is scheduled to be transported to a massive landfill in less than three hours. If we don't recover the urn before then, we may never be able to find it."

Not wasting a minute, Trini teleported to an alleyway behind a shopping mall in downtown Tokyo. It was early in the morning, but the mall was already bustling with activity. She looked around to make sure nobody was watching and then squeezed through a gap under a fence. A wretched stench hit her senses like a slap in the face when she emerged on the other side. She took a quick look around and was startled to see that there wasn't just one Dumpster; there were hundreds.

"Alpha 5, are you seeing what I'm seeing?" Trini asked.

"Aye-yi-yi, I'm sorry, Trini," Alpha 5 said. "When we first detected the Dumpster, it was in an isolated location. The mall workers must have moved it."

Trini pinched her nose to block out the stench. "Any clue which Dumpster the urn is in?"

"Not precisely, but I know it's somewhere in your immediate area," Alpha 5 said.

"In that case, I've got just one thing to say." Trini pulled out her Morpher. "It's Morphin Time!"

One after another, the Yellow Ranger flipped open the lids of the Dumpsters, hoping to find the one containing the urn. Most of the Dumpsters were filled to the brim with molding food and other assorted garbage.

"Alpha 5, I could search all day and not find the

urn. There has to be a way to narrow the search," the Yellow Ranger said.

"Perhaps you should just ask the cats," a snarly voice said from behind her.

The Yellow Ranger yelped, then spun around. Standing atop a Dumpster was a hairy creature with the body of a woman and the head of a cat.

"Just a friendly neighborhood alley cat," it said.

The Yellow Ranger took a cautious step back. "I remember learning about a mythical cat at the museum. That's you, right?"

"Now that's not a very nice way to talk about your new friend," the cat scoffed in offense. "I do have a name, you know."

"I didn't know we were friends. But maybe we should start with introductions. You can call me the Yellow Ranger," Trini said.

The cat sneered. "That's not a name! That's a warrior title!"

"A title I'm really proud to have," the Yellow Ranger said. "So what do I call you?"

"Since you asked so nicely," the cat said, glaring ominously at the Yellow Ranger, "the name is Bastet, or at least it is for the sake of this conversation."

"Nice to meet you, Bastet," the Yellow Ranger said, not daring to take her eyes off the creature for even a second. "Maybe you can help me out. I'm looking for an urn. It's red and about half as tall as we are."

"And so much for us being friends," Bastet said, giving her a dangerous snarl.

The Yellow Ranger's adrenaline was rising fast. "I'm guessing you're the guardian of the urn, and that means we're about to have a fight."

Bastet raised her hands, revealing ten razor-sharp claws sticking out from her fingertips. "It's not that I wouldn't enjoy shredding you into kitty litter, but fighting just isn't my thing. I'm more interested in playing a little game called 'catch me if you can.'"

"And why would I play such a game with you?" the Yellow Ranger asked.

"Because I have this," Bastet said, clicking her claws together. In a flash, the red urn appeared in her arms. In a swift bound, she took off running.

"I should have seen that coming," the Yellow Ranger said, letting out a long sigh.

And with that, the chase was on.

Chapter 21

With the red urn clutched under one arm, Bastet leaped from one Dumpster to the next. Her catlike agility made it tough for the Yellow Ranger to keep up the chase. Every time she got close to catching Bastet, the cunning creature dashed off in another direction.

"Catch me if you can, Yellow Ranger," Bastet teased.

"Oh, I'm going to catch you, and when I do—" The Yellow Ranger then lost her footing on a mess of garbage. She tumbled from the top of a Dumpster and flopped down onto the asphalt.

Bastet glanced down at the Yellow Ranger from atop a Dumpster. "You may have the agility of a cat, but you sure don't have our pizzazz."

The Yellow Ranger rolled to her feet and grabbed her blade blaster. Taking quick aim, she squeezed off several rounds. Bastet nimbly flipped and cartwheeled around, dodging every shot.

"Now that wasn't friendly at all," Bastet snarled and landed on the exact point where she had started. "So tell me, Yellow Ranger, why do you want this old urn, anyway?"

"I just do, so why not hand it over?" Trini said, keeping her blaster aimed at Bastet.

"You must have a better reason than that." Bastet clicked her claws together. "Is this about a boy?"

The Yellow Ranger rolled her eyes in irritation. "Not in the way you mean, if you mean what I think you mean."

"So what you're really saying is, the boy in the urn put you in the friend zone. Too bad! So sad!" Bastet teased.

The Yellow Ranger scowled. "It's so not like that. He's the Red Power Ranger and the leader of my team."

Bastet giggled. "That was so much easier to get out of you than I expected. And now that I know, you're never getting him back," she said, then clicked her claws. The urn vanished in a flickering flash. She then dashed away with the lightning-quick speed of a cheetah.

The Yellow Ranger grunted in frustration and raced after her. Bastet reached the perimeter fence and sprang high into the air, clearing it in an effortless bound. The Yellow Ranger proved to be equally agile and leaped over the fence with the same ease. When she hit the ground on the other side, she saw Bastet was still on the run and already over fifty yards away.

"Alpha 5, I've found the urn, but its guardian creature is crazy quick. Is there any way you can track the thing?" the Yellow Ranger asked.

"Aye-yi-yi, I'll do my best," said Alpha 5.

The Yellow Ranger chased Bastet down an alleyway, across a parking lot, and onto a busy city street. They nimbly dashed and weaved around pedestrians on the crowded sidewalks. People watched in amazement, snapping photos and recording videos.

The Yellow Ranger rounded a street corner. Bastet was nowhere to be seen. "Alpha 5, I've lost her. Any idea where she went?"

"She's at an intersection two blocks from your position," Alpha 5 replied. "Hold on for an assist."

Alpha 5 teleported the Yellow Ranger to Bastet's location. Upon her arrival, the Yellow Ranger heard horns honking and tires screeching. She then saw Bastet crossing the street by nimbly leaping from the top of one speeding car to the next.

The Yellow Ranger looked for an opening to safely cross, but there were far too many speeding cars in her way. "Alpha 5, I could use another assist."

Alpha 5 teleported the Yellow Ranger to the other side of the street. She emerged just ahead of Bastet. The clever creature hissed viciously and skidded to a stop.

"The yellow kitty's more cunning than I thought," Bastet said. "Now let's find out if she can climb like a real cat." She whisked past the Yellow Ranger and swiftly scurried up the side of a building.

"That is way beyond my climbing skills," the Yellow Ranger said.

"I've got you covered, Trini," said Alpha 5.

Alpha 5 teleported the Yellow Ranger to the building's rooftop, just as Bastet completed her climb and leaped up onto the ledge.

"Miss me?" the Yellow Ranger asked.

Bastet screeched with fright and nearly tumbled over the ledge.

The Yellow Ranger grabbed her by the leg just in time. "Saved your life."

Bastet pulled away. "I suppose I should thank you for that."

The Yellow Ranger wheezed to catch her breath. "The way I see it, we can either keep up this chase forever, fight it out for the urn, or come up with a third option."

Bastet grinned deviously. "How about we play a new game? I ask you three riddles, and if you get them all right, you can have the urn."

The Yellow Ranger eyed Bastet skeptically. "I suspect a trick, but I'm game if you are."

"Oh goody, I so love a good game of riddles." Bastet tapped her forehead with a claw tip as she thought up a riddle. "Riddle one: There are two sisters. One gives birth to the other and she, in turn, gives birth to the first. Who are the sisters?"

Trini grinned, having remembered learning this riddle several years ago while on an Angel Scout trip. "Easy! Night and day."

Bastet grimaced in irritation. "Riddle two: What walks on four legs in the morning, two in the afternoon, and three at night?"

Trini snickered. "Also easy. The answer is a person. We crawl on all fours as babies, then walk on two legs as adults and three when we get old and have to use a cane."

Bastet gritted her teeth. "Now for riddle three. I must warn you that this one might send you plunging head over heels. Are you sure you want to risk it?"

"Just get to it. I've got places to be," the Yellow Ranger said.

"As you wish," Bastet said. "Riddle three: What can both blind a person and make her see?"

The Yellow Ranger remembered hearing this riddle on a cartoon she had seen as a little girl. "The answer is sand. If it gets in your eyes, you won't be able to see, but sand can also be ground up to make glass for glasses."

Bastet purred. "Very well done, Yellow Ranger. I am indeed impressed."

"I've played your game, so give me the urn as we agreed," the Yellow Ranger demanded.

"Of course, Yellow Ranger," Bastet said, then clicked her claws. The red urn appeared in her hands. "But first, I have a bonus riddle for you. What game do cats hate but dogs adore?"

The Yellow Ranger shrugged, not quite certain. "Is it 'go fetch'?"

"It is 'go fetch,'" Bastet said with a giggle, then flung the urn as hard as she could, right over the ledge of the building. "So go fetch, kitty."

"I should have seen that coming," the Yellow Ranger said. She fearlessly raced for the ledge and dove off the building. Plummeting headfirst toward the pavement, she reached out for the urn.

Mere seconds before impact, the Yellow Ranger caught the urn and rotated to get her feet beneath her. She hit the ground, then skillfully managed to execute a dazzling dive roll, and sprang to her feet. She stood, gasping to catch her breath. She was stunned that she'd been able to perform such a dazzling feat.

"That was amazing, Trini," Alpha 5 cheered. "I guess it is true what they say: Cats really do always land on their feet."

Chapter 22

At the Command Center, Trini carefully placed the red urn on a workbench next to the other three. A tear trickled down her cheek when she saw the four urns together. It reminded her of just how much she missed her friends.

Alpha 5 placed a hand on Trini's shoulder to comfort her. "Don't be sad. We're going to find a way to get them out of there."

Trini wiped a tear from her eye. "The Griffin Pharaoh's nano-solidification is only a day from being complete. Once that happens, they may be stuck in there forever."

Zordon looked down at Trini. "There may be a solution, but it is potentially dangerous."

"Aye-yi-yi! Don't tell me you're thinking what I think you're thinking," said Alpha 5.

"It may be our last chance to save the Rangers. We have to try," Zordon said.

"What are you two talking about?" Trini asked nervously.

Alpha 5 brought up a digital display of the Command Center on a computer screen. "The idea would be to channel energy from Zordon's hyperspace chamber into the Command Center's teleportation matrix. That could make it possible to extract the Rangers from the urns."

"So what's the dangerous part of this plan?" Trini asked.

"Zordon's connection to the Command Center could become destabilized. If that happens, he could be lost forever," Alpha 5 said.

Trini shook her head. "Zordon, you can't seriously be considering this."

"If there is even the slightest possibility of success, we have to try," Zordon said. "Alpha 5, prepare the transporter's power buffers."

"Whatever you say, Zordon," Alpha 5 said.

"Trini, if this doesn't work, you must flee the Command Center with the utmost haste," Zordon warned.

Trini took a nervous gulp and nodded.

"We'll start with the lowest power setting,"

Alpha 5 said. He flicked a series of switches on the main computer console. "Engaging power transfer now."

An energy field started to swirl around the urns, causing them to glow. Trini's eyes lit up with joy when she saw faint outlines of the Rangers trapped inside.

"We've breached the exterior shells. Increasing power," Alpha 5 said, turning a dial on the console from 25 percent to 50 percent.

The urns began to shimmy and shake.

"I think it's working," Trini said excitedly. "Try increasing the power again."

"I'm not sure that's a good idea," Alpha 5 said. "I'm picking up irregularities in the containment field."

Inside the hyperspace chamber, Zordon began to flicker slightly. "The irregularities are within safety parameters. You may proceed, but please do so with extreme caution."

"Aye-yi-yi, I hope you're right about this, Zordon," Alpha 5 said, increasing power to 75 percent.

The energy field swirled faster and faster. The urns shook harder. The lids clanked and clunked. Trini was certain the tops were going to burst open and the Rangers would be freed.

"Increasing to maximum power," Alpha 5 said, turning the dial to 100 percent.

Searing bolts of energy zapped from the urns. Trini and Alpha 5 had to dive for cover to avoid getting shocked. Several of the control consoles took direct hits, shorting them out. Inside the hyperspace chamber, Zordon disappeared and reappeared over and over again.

"We have to shut it down before the Command Center is destroyed," Trini shouted.

"Aye-yi-yi, I knew this was a bad idea," Alpha 5 said, reaching for the power dial, but a bolt of energy zapped him. He stumbled backward and fell to the floor. "Systems overload. Must shut down and reboot." He then went offline.

"Trini, you must abandon the Command Center. Save yourself," Zordon said. He was in danger of disappearing entirely.

Trini wasn't about to leave her friends again. Taking a deep breath, she gathered her courage and dashed toward the main console. She dodged the blistering energy bolts and leaped toward the console, slamming down her hand on the shutdown switch.

The energy field dispersed. The glow around the

urns faded away. The energy bolts stopped blasting from the urns. Zordon stabilized and returned to his normal state. Alpha 5 finished rebooting and sat holding his head in bewildered confusion.

"Trini, are you okay?" Zordon asked.

Trini nodded. "I'm fine. But it looks like the Rangers may stay trapped forever."

"Don't give up, Trini," Zordon said. "We will find another way. I promise."

Chapter 23

That night at Angel Grove Park, the Griffin Pharaoh strutted around arrogantly. He approached the playground that Trini had picked for the Community Fix Up. The monkey bars, slides, and swings were bent, twisted, and broken, the unfortunate result of a recent attack by the evil forces of Rita Repulsa.

"This will be the perfect spot for my new pyramid, but first I need to clear out this junk," the Griffin Pharaoh said, raising his cyclone staff. It began to spin rapidly, causing a massive gust of wind. Piece by piece, the remains of the damaged playground were blown away into the distance.

"Now I just need a legion of servants to build the thing," the Griffin Pharaoh said. He looked at his hands. The Nanosand was hardly moving. "In just one more day, I'll be indestructible. Then the world will be mine to rule."

A bright light flashed nearby. The Griffin Pharaoh

turned and shielded his eyes from the burning glare. When the light had faded away, Finster stood holding a red velvet pillow with the mind-control crown atop it. Squatt and Baboo stood cowering behind him.

The Griffin Pharaoh pointed his staff at them. "Stay back, peasants. I have grown weary of your foolish antics."

Finster bowed down on one knee. "My most sincere apologies, master. We are here to pledge our allegiance to your greatness." He approached the Griffin Pharaoh and presented the crown. "And to prove our worth, we have brought a gift for you."

The Griffin Pharaoh leaned in for a closer look. "What exactly is this strange trinket?"

"It's your new crown," Finster said. "All great rulers should have one, and you are the greatest ruler of all."

"That's not true," Squatt said with a raised fist. "Queen Rita is the greatest ruler in the whole universe."

"And when she gets back from her secret trip, she'll prove it," Squatt said.

The Griffin Pharaoh glared at them bitterly. "What treachery is this?"

Finster gritted his teeth. "Ignore those oafs. They're just too foolish to recognize your greatness.

Now may I place this crown upon your head?"

The Griffin Pharaoh nodded. "Very well. You may have the honor."

Finster stepped behind the Griffin Pharaoh and placed the crown upon his head. "A perfect fit. Now everyone will know who's in charge."

"You have served me well, little peasant," said the Griffin Pharaoh.

"Oh, you'll find I am far more than a peasant," Finster said. From his back pocket, he pulled out a crudely built remote control with blinking lights and a long antenna. He turned a large knob and flicked a few switches on the device. "Now you're going to serve me. Isn't that right?"

The lights on the crown blinked red. The Griffin Pharaoh's eyes glazed over with a vacant expression. He was suddenly in a hypnotic trance. "Yes, master, I will serve you."

"We did it," Squatt cheered.

"Now we can finally get our plan back on track," Baboo said.

Squatt and Baboo grabbed for the remote control.

Finster stepped back. "Watch it, you fools. This device is much too delicate for your clumsy hands.

I will handle things from here. And the first thing we need to do is trap the Yellow Ranger in the fifth urn."

"And where and how are we going to do that?" Squatt asked.

Finster walked over to a lamppost and looked at a sign advertising the Community Fix Up. At the bottom of the sign, it read: HOSTED BY TRINI KWAN AND THE ANGEL SCOUTS, SATURDAY AT 8:00 A.M. "The when and where will be right here," he said, grinning maliciously.

Chapter 24

Dawn hadn't yet broken when Trini arrived at Angel Grove Park. After days of mishaps and missteps on her Angel Scout leadership exam, she knew the Community Fix Up was her last chance to prove herself to Ms. Gertrude. Nothing on earth would stand between her and a successful event.

Trini's hopeful outlook on the day came crashing down when she arrived at the playground. Every last piece of the equipment had vanished. Little did she know, the Griffin Pharaoh had sent it all soaring to distant areas of the park.

"Alpha 5, do you read me?" Trini said into her communicator.

"I'm receiving you, Trini. It took a lot of work, but most of the Command Center's systems are back online," Alpha 5 said.

"That's great news," Trini said. "If the viewing globe is working, please take a quick look around

Angel Grove Park and tell me if you see anything out of the ordinary."

"Will do," Alpha 5 said. A minute passed before he spoke again. "Aye-yi-yi! There are pieces of broken playground equipment scattered all over the park. How could that have happened?"

Trini sighed. "No idea, but I need to get all those pieces to the playground before the Fix Up begins."

"I'm not sure that you could do that even if you had a week. Some of those pieces weigh hundreds of pounds," said Alpha 5.

"There's only one way I could do it," Trini said. "Zordon, do you hear me?"

"I do, Trini. And while I don't condone the use of Ranger powers for personal gain, I am always in favor of helping the people of Angel Grove," said Zordon.

Trini morphed into the Yellow Ranger and got to work. With Alpha 5 guiding the way, she was able to locate the missing pieces of equipment. For the next two hours, she carried, pushed, and dragged every piece back to the playground. She moved slides, swings, and monkey bars. Even with her powers, the process was frustratingly difficult and dreadfully exhausting.

By the time sunrise arrived, she had managed

to recover the majority of the pieces and parts. She could only hope that her team of volunteers would be able to put the piles of rubble back together. A mere minute after she de-morphed and sat down to catch her breath, Ms. Gertrude arrived.

"Ms. Kwan, I'm pleased to see you here this early," said Ms. Gertrude. She looked over the mess of rubble and wrote a note on her clipboard. "You've sure got your work cut out for you today. I do hope you're up for it?"

Trini nodded with certainty. "You better believe I am."

An hour later, the mangled playground was abuzz with activity. Dozens of volunteers arrived to help out. Some brought tools and construction equipment, while others brought food and drinks to keep everyone going. Trini raced around tirelessly to keep everything organized.

By late morning, the volunteers were working together like a well-oiled machine. With Trini leading the effort, there was little doubt that the work would be completed in a single day. Making it even better, Ms. Gertrude was quite pleased with the results and even complimented Trini on her organizational skills.

When noon rolled around and everyone broke for lunch, Trini got a chance to rest. She tried to enjoy her moment of success, but it wasn't easy knowing that the other Rangers were still trapped inside the urns. If that wasn't stressful enough, the Griffin Pharaoh was mere minutes from completing nano-solidification, and she had no idea how to find him, much less defeat him.

Silvia dropped a heavy history book on the table in front of Trini. "I have great news. Can you guess what it is?"

Startled, Trini leaped halfway out of her seat. "Silvia, I didn't notice you there."

"Sorry, I just had to tell you right away." Silvia flipped open the book to the chapter about the Griffin Pharaoh. "I figured out his weakness. It was right here in the book all along."

Just then, startled screams erupted from all around. The scouts and volunteers were scattering in a panic. Trini saw the cause of the chaos: An army of Putty Patrollers swarmed into the area. Squatt and Baboo then teleported into the middle of the playground.

"Putty Patrollers, capture the humans. Don't let any escape," Squatt commanded.

Chapter 25

"Trini, what do we do?" Silvia cried.

Trini knew the Putty Patrollers were far too great in number for her to fight alone. They were already rounding up the scouts and volunteers and herding them into the center of the playground. Her only chance would be to morph into the Yellow Ranger, but that wasn't an option with so many people around.

Before Trini could figure out a plan, a pair of Putty Patrollers raced her way. The first grabbed Trini from behind and locked its muscular arms around her waist. The other Putty Patroller scooped up Silvia over its shoulder. She screamed and kicked helplessly, trying to get away.

"Let her go," Trini yelled. With a powerful backward thrust, she jammed an elbow into the gut of her Putty captor. The thing doubled over and lost its grip on her. Trini then spun around and pummeled it with several punches to the chest. The Putty flickered and vanished.

"Trini, help me," Silvia cried as the other Putty Patroller carried her away toward the playground.

"Hold on, Silvia, I'm coming," Trini shouted.

Just as Trini was about to chase after Silvia, Zordon called on the communicator.

"Trini, you cannot pursue the Putty. The chance of being captured is much too great," Zordon said.

"I can't just leave Silvia," Trini protested.

"And you can't help anyone if you're captured. You must escape now while you still can," Zordon insisted.

The Putty Patroller carrying Silvia reached the playground and dropped her in the sand. Ms. Gertrude pulled Silvia close and told her to hold hands with the other scouts.

The situation then went from bad to worse. In a whirlwind of smoke and lightning, the Griffin Pharaoh appeared. The mind-control crown was still on top of his head. Finster stood by his side, commanding him with the remote control.

"Greetings, peasants, I am your new master," the Griffin Pharaoh said.

"Trini, you can delay no longer," Zordon said.

Trini knew Zordon was right. Wiping a tear from her eye, she took off running as fast as she could. It took her a couple of minutes to reach an area with trees and heavy bushes where she could hide. She first looked back to make sure none of the Putty Patrollers had followed her and then took cover deep in the foliage.

Wheezing to catch her breath, Trini did her best not to think about the hopelessness of the situation. "Zordon, there's no way to defeat the Griffin Pharaoh on my own," Trini said into her communicator. "How much longer until his nano-solidification is complete?"

"Minutes at best," Zordon said.

"Aye-yi-yi," Alpha 5 said. "I've been trying to find a weakness we could use against him, but I still haven't figured anything out."

Trini suddenly recalled her talk with Silvia before the attack. "Silvia may know the answer. She was trying to tell me about a weakness she had discovered in her mythology book."

"Then we must get that book right away," Zordon said.

"There's no time for that. I'll have to ask her myself," Trini said, with newfound determination.

Chapter 26

At the playground, the Putty Patrollers swarmed around the hostages, making sure they couldn't escape. Ms. Gertrude and the Angel Scouts cowered together fearfully with the rest of the volunteers.

Silvia, unlike the rest, wasn't frightened at all. "Don't worry. The Power Rangers will be here soon."

Daisy, who was scared to tears, locked her arms around Silvia and held on tight.

Nearby, Squatt and Baboo approached Finster and the Griffin Pharaoh.

"We have all the hostages, but we don't see the Yellow Ranger," Squatt said.

"She'll be here soon enough," Finster said. He then took a close look at the Griffin Pharaoh's hands. The Nanosand was hardly moving. The nano-solidification process was nearly complete. "And when she arrives, there will be nothing she can do to stop us."

"I hope you're right, because here she comes,"

Baboo said to his evil crew.

The Yellow Ranger dashed across the grassy field. Upon reaching the playground, she attacked the Putty Patrollers, unleashing a barrage of walloping punches and spinning kicks. She took out two Putty Patrollers with a leaping split kick, then demolished another with a backflip kick. Other Putty Patrollers tried to grab her arms and legs, but the Yellow Ranger would not be stopped.

Silvia cheered gleefully. "I told you the Power Rangers would come."

Daisy smiled half-heartedly. "I see one, but where are the others?"

A dozen Putty Patrollers surrounded the Yellow Ranger. Deploying her Power Daggers, she thrust her arms outward, reducing two Putty Patrollers to dust. She then quickly hacked the others to pieces.

"Quite impressive, Yellow Ranger," the Griffin Pharaoh said. "It seems you are worthy to battle me."

"Then face me one-on-one, unless you're a coward," the Yellow Ranger said.

"I am no coward," the Griffin Pharaoh said, raising his fists. "I will destroy you and all memory of your feeble existence."

"Oh no, you will not," Finster said, flicking switches on the remote control. "I ordered you to capture the Yellow Ranger in the fifth urn."

"I will not be ordered around—" the Griffin Pharaoh said, trying to resist, but he lost control when the lights on his crown flashed red. "Yes, Master Finster, I will capture the Yellow Ranger."

The Yellow Ranger noticed the crown atop the Griffin Pharaoh's head. "Zordon, any idea what that thing is?"

"Without proper analysis I can only speculate, though it appears to be some sort of mind-control device," Zordon said.

"And I bet Finster is controlling him with that remote," Alpha 5 said.

The Griffin Pharaoh pointed his cyclone staff at the fifth urn. The top hinged open, and the ominous shadow-hand arose from inside. "Now, Yellow Ranger, you will be my prisoner for all time."

The Yellow Ranger watched fearfully as the shadow-hand slowly began to move her way. "You'll have to catch me first."

Finster grinned. "That is where you are mistaken. You're going to allow yourself to be captured."

The Yellow Ranger scoffed. "And why would I ever do that?"

Finster flicked the switches on the remote control. The Griffin Pharaoh, in turn, reacted by pointing his cyclone staff toward the hostages on the playground. The shadow-hand changed course and began to head in their direction. "Because if you refuse, one of your precious scouts will be going in your place," Finster said.

Chapter 27

The Yellow Ranger watched in terror as the shadow-hand moved ever closer to the playground. Ms. Gertrude stood trembling with her arms extended, doing her best to protect the scouts. Silvia and Daisy held hands and covered their eyes.

"Zordon, I have to surrender," the Yellow Ranger said.

"If you do that, there may never be a way to set you free from the urn," Zordon warned.

Finster looked at the Yellow Ranger. "You have the power to stop this, Yellow Ranger."

The Yellow Ranger saw the shadow-hand closing in on the scouts. "Fine. Finster, you win."

Squatt raised a fist in anger. "Stop giving Finster all the credit. This is our plan and our win."

Baboo bucked up his chest. "And we should be the ones controlling the Griffin Pharaoh."

Squatt and Baboo then tried to grab the remote

control back from Finster's grasp.

"Stay back, you fools. You'll ruin everything," Finster said, trying to swat them away, and in doing so, he dropped the remote.

The red lights on the Griffin Pharaoh's crown faded. He ambled around in confusion. "What is happening here?"

"Trini, now is your chance," Zordon said. "Destroy the crown before the Griffin Pharaoh comes to his senses."

The Yellow Ranger drew her blade blaster and took aim at the Griffin Pharaoh's crown. She squeezed off two shots, but in the same instant, he stumbled to the side, causing the shots to hit him in the chest and shoulder.

The Griffin Pharaoh looked down at his body. There wasn't a bit of damage, and the Nanosand had stopped moving entirely. The nano-solidification was complete. "I am invincible," he shouted.

Squatt picked up the remote control and flicked the switches. "And we'll be the ones controlling you."

Baboo grabbed for the remote control. "Stop hogging it. Give me a chance."

Finster also tried to grab for the remote. "You're

going to break it, you idiots."

The red lights on the Griffin Pharaoh's crown flickered on and off. He stumbled around in confusion. At the same time, the shadow-hand floated around in random directions.

The Yellow Ranger aimed her blade blaster at the Griffin Pharaoh and fired two more shots, but he was stumbling around so much that it caused her to miss the crown by inches.

The Griffin Pharaoh roared furiously. "I've had enough of you, Yellow Ranger," he said, then pointed his cyclone staff in her direction. The shadow-hand turned and headed her way.

The Yellow Ranger leaped clear just as the shadow-hand tried to grab her. Again she aimed the blade blaster at the Griffin Pharaoh's crown and fired several more shots. The Griffin Pharaoh spun his cyclone staff, deflecting the bolts.

In the same instant, the fifth urn flickered and faded for a brief moment.

"Zordon, did you see that?" the Yellow Ranger asked.

"I did, and there was a similar reaction with the urns here," Zordon said. "Perhaps his staff is somehow the key to opening the urns."

"Then I need to find a way to destroy that thing," the Yellow Ranger said.

"Aye-yi-yi, Trini, look out," Alpha 5 cried.

The Yellow Ranger looked back just in time to see the shadow-hand trying to grab her. She dive-rolled away, again barely evading capture.

Finster managed to grab the remote control from Squatt. "Now let's end this mess before it gets any worse," he said, flicking the switches on the remote.

The Yellow Ranger looked at Finster and realized she'd been going about this all wrong. She took aim at the remote control. With a squeeze of the trigger, she blasted the thing into a thousand pieces. Finster shielded his face and stumbled backward.

The lights on the Griffin Pharaoh's crown faded. "You fools were using this to control me," he said, pulling the crown from his head and smashing it on the ground.

"Uh-oh," Squatt and Baboo said, looking fearfully at each other.

The Yellow Ranger raised a fist at the Griffin Pharaoh. "Now will you fight me one-on-one?"

"I've grown weary of this nonsense," the Griffin

Pharaoh said, then angled his staff toward the Yellow Ranger. The shadow-hand began to move toward her. "Perhaps I will give you a chance in ninety-nine years!"

"Yellow Ranger! Look out!" Silvia shouted from the playground.

The Yellow Ranger looked back just as the shadow-hand swooped in and grabbed her. She flailed and kicked her legs, but she couldn't break free. The shadow-hand then began to carry her toward the fifth urn.

"Trini, try targeting the Griffin Pharaoh's staff with your blade blaster. It may be your only chance," Zordon said.

The Yellow Ranger aimed her blade blaster at the cyclone staff and started firing as fast as she could. The staff was a small target, so most of the shots missed, but one shot hit the staff in the very center. The shadow-hand's grip on her weakened.

The fifth urn briefly faded away.

"It's working. Keep firing," Alpha 5 cheered.

The shadow-hand was only feet from the urn. The Yellow Ranger fired several more shots, this time landing two at the end of the staff. The shadow-hand's grip grew weaker, though not enough for the Yellow Ranger to break free.

The Griffin Pharaoh laughed triumphantly. "You'll never escape my grasp, Yellow Ranger."

"The blaster isn't doing enough damage. I have to try something else," the Yellow Ranger said, dropping her blade blaster.

"Aye-yi-yi, what are you doing, Trini?" Alpha 5 asked.

"The only thing I can do," the Yellow Ranger said, and then deployed her Power Daggers. "And if it doesn't work, this will be the end of the Power Rangers."

Chapter 28

With only seconds left before being pulled into the fifth urn, the Yellow Ranger tightened her grip on the Power Daggers. "You're going down, Griffin Pharaoh."

"Hit me with your best shot, Yellow Ranger," the Griffin Pharaoh said.

The Yellow Ranger took a deep breath and flung a Power Dagger with all her might. The dagger soared at supersonic speed, hitting the center of the cyclone staff. Blazing sparks blasted out in every direction. The staff cracked down the center, though it remained in one piece. The shadow-hand vanished, causing the Yellow Ranger to flop to the ground.

For a brief instant, the fifth urn vanished completely.

"Great hit," Alpha 5 cheered.

Zordon said, "Trini, I am now certain that if you destroy the cyclone staff, the other Rangers will be set free."

"That's all I needed to hear," the Yellow Ranger said. She then glanced back at the scouts and volunteers. "It's time for you to get out of here. Run straight for town, and don't look back."

"Thank you, Ms. Yellow Ranger," Ms. Gertrude said, then began to lead the scouts away.

"We can't go yet." Silvia pulled away and ran toward the edge of the playground. "Hey, Yellow Ranger, the Griffin Pharaoh is made of sand and stone, so he doesn't like water. Get him wet, and he'll start to fall to pieces."

Ms. Gertrude took Silvia by the hand and led her away.

Nearby, Finster slumped in defeat. "Our hostages are escaping. How could this get any worse?"

"It's going to be a lot worse when Rita gets here," Squatt said.

Finster gasped fearfully. "And when will that be?"

Squatt and Baboo cringed nervously.

Zordon called the Yellow Ranger on her communicator. "Trini, if Silvia is correct about water, your best chance will be to get the Griffin Pharaoh near the lake."

"I'll add that to my to-do list, but first things first.

It's time to free the other Rangers," the Yellow Ranger said, raising a fist. She then charged the Griffin Pharaoh head-on and attacked him with a barrage of punches and kicks, trying with all her might to hit his staff. He blocked and dodged every strike, just managing to keep the staff out of her reach.

The Griffin Pharaoh bashed the Yellow Ranger with a walloping back fist, knocking her to the ground. "When are you going to learn that I am invincible?"

As the Yellow Ranger crawled to her feet, she noticed a sprinkler head in the grass. She then looked around and saw sprinklers all over. "Alpha 5, any chance you can use the Command Center's computer to access the park's irrigation system?"

"Great idea, Trini! Keep him busy while I work it out," Alpha 5 replied.

The Yellow Ranger gasped for breath as she pushed up to her feet. Again she attacked the Griffin Pharaoh with a series of kicks and punches, but her strikes didn't do a bit of damage. "Alpha 5, I don't know how much longer I can keep this up."

"Let's see if this helps," Alpha 5 replied.

Dozens of sprinklers sprang to life and began spraying water in every direction. The Yellow Ranger smiled as she watched the water rain down on the Griffin Pharaoh. His rock-solid muscles began to turn into mush like wet sand. His legs wobbled and weakened until he could no longer stand, and finally he stumbled to his knees.

"What's happening to me?" the Griffin Pharaoh wailed.

"You're going down, is what's happening," the Yellow Ranger said, attacking him again. She punched and kicked him with all the strength she could muster. Every strike caused him to grunt and groan. Bits of gold and rock cracked off his arms as he blocked her strikes. She then delivered a jumping spin-kick, bashing him across the face and sending him crashing to the ground.

"And now it's time to free the other Rangers," the Yellow Ranger said. She yanked the cyclone staff out of the Griffin Pharaoh's weakened hands and cracked it across her knee, breaking it into two pieces. A blazing bolt of energy shot out of the mangled staff, zapping her right off her feet.

Chapter 29

"You did it, Trini. The other Rangers are free," Alpha 5 cheered over the communicator.

"That's great news," the Yellow Ranger said, too exhausted even to smile. "Please tell them I could really use some support."

"They'll be heading to your location shortly," Alpha 5 said.

Nearby, the Griffin Pharaoh was clawing and crawling through the wet grass, trying desperately to get away. "I was wrong to underestimate your power, Yellow Ranger. I am defeated."

A bright light flashed nearby. The Yellow Ranger turned and was startled to see that Rita Repulsa had just teleported into the area. The evil witch held a golden staff with a crescent moon mounted to the top.

"I leave for a few days, and look at the chaos my stupid minions have unleashed," Rita shrilled.

Finster hurried over and kneeled down before

Rita. "My queen, before you get too angry, please let me explain."

"It was Finster's fault," Squatt said as he and Baboo raced over.

"He talked us into the whole thing," said Baboo.

Rita bashed the three of them on their heads with her staff. "I don't care whose fault it was. I'll make you all suffer when we get back to the Moon Palace."

The Yellow Ranger trembled nervously. "Zordon, things just went from bad to worse. I could use the help of the other Rangers."

"Ask and you shall receive," Zordon said.

In a flash of red, blue, black, and pink, the other Power Rangers appeared.

"You have no idea how happy I am to see you all," said the Yellow Ranger.

"We wouldn't be here if it wasn't for you," said the Red Ranger.

Rita rolled her eyes in disgust. "So sorry to break up your happy reunion, but I hate to see a good monster go to waste," she said, then spiked her staff into the ground. Bolts of mystical energy blasted through the grass and traveled to the Griffin Pharaoh. "Make my monster grow!"

The mystical energy surged through the Griffin Pharaoh, causing him to grow and grow until he stood fifty feet tall. He extended an arm and his cyclone staff appeared in his hand, again unbroken.

"We need Dinozord power!" the Red Ranger shouted and raised his fist to the sky. "Tyrannosaurus Dinozord Power!"

The other Rangers also raised their fists.

"Mastodon Dinozord Power!" said the Black Ranger.

"Pterodactyl Dinozord Power!" said the Pink Ranger.

"Sabertooth Tiger Dinozord Power!" said the Yellow Ranger.

"Triceratops Dinozord Power!" said the Blue Ranger.

Arising from distant corners of the world, the five robotic Dinozords emerged from their secret lairs. Moments later, they arrived in Angel Grove, roaring furiously and primed for battle. The five Rangers leaped high in the air and landed in the cockpits of the mighty machines.

"Now it's time for Megazord action," the Yellow Ranger shouted.

The five Dinozords began combining into a single robotic machine. The Sabertooth Tiger and Triceratops became the legs. The Mastodon transformed into a pair of hulking arms. The Tyrannosaurus became the torso that interlinked all the parts. The Pterodactyl took the form of an armored chest plate and merged with the mighty machine. Once complete, the Megazord towered over 150 feet high and weighed over one hundred tons.

All five Rangers emerged in a single command cockpit.

"Let's finish off this jerk," the Yellow Ranger said. "And let's try not to totally trash the park while doing it."

The Griffin Pharaoh attacked first, swinging his staff at the Megazord, scoring a thunderous strike. The Megazord counterattacked with a series of punches, causing the Griffin Pharaoh to stumble backward.

The Griffin Pharaoh held out his cyclone staff. It fanned around rapidly, creating a massive gust of wind. The Megazord had to strain with all its might to avoid getting blown away.

"We have to do something about that staff," the Yellow Ranger said. She flicked a series of switches on the control console. "Firing rockets."

A dozen rockets shot from the Megazord and hit the Griffin Pharaoh's staff. The explosive assault forced him to retreat several steps back. One of his massive feet stepped right on the newly rebuilt playground.

The Yellow Ranger shook her fist. "Now I'm really mad. Let's make him pay for that."

The Red Ranger raised a hand skyward. "I call on the Power Sword!"

A gleaming sword appeared in the Megazord's hand. The mighty machine then unleashed several Power Sword swipes at the Griffin Pharaoh, forcing him to block with his staff. Every strike sent sparks exploding from the staff until, at last, the Megazord hacked it in half.

"You may have destroyed my staff, but I am invincible," the Griffin Pharaoh bellowed.

"That's what you think," the Yellow Ranger shouted. "Team, we need to get him to the lake."

The Megazord dashed toward the Griffin Pharaoh and locked its massive arms around him. Heaving him off his feet, the Megazord began to trek toward the lake on the far side of the park. The Griffin Pharaoh flailed helplessly.

The Yellow Ranger cringed when she saw that the

Megazord was stomping huge footprints in the grass. "We're going to need a lot of volunteers to fix up this mess."

The Megazord reached the lake and dropped the Griffin Pharaoh right next to the shore.

"I am the great Griffin Pharaoh. You'll never destroy me," he shouted.

"Think again," the Yellow Ranger said, giving her control stick a hard thrust forward.

The Megazord's right leg, formed from the Yellow Ranger's Sabertooth Tiger Zord, swung back and then kicked the Griffin Pharaoh in the chest. The devastating blow knocked the brute off his feet and sent him tumbling backward, leaving him standing knee-deep in the water.

The Griffin Pharaoh wailed as his legs rapidly dissolved. The Nanosand scattered and sunk lifelessly into the depths of the lake. Unable to remain standing, he stumbled onto his hands and knees. He thrashed around trying to escape, but his arms dissolved too. Soon after, his torso sunk beneath the water and, finally, his head.

Nearby, Rita screeched in furious rage. "That was a huge waste of my time. Just wait until I get you all back to the Moon Palace."

Rita, Finster, Squatt, and Baboo vanished in a flickering flash.

In the Megazord, the Yellow Ranger breathed a huge sigh of relief. It was finally over.

"You did it, Trini. You saved us all," said the Red Ranger.

"You all would have done the same for me," the Yellow Ranger said. "And if you want to make it up to me, I could really use a big ice cream sundae."

The Rangers all laughed, once again reunited as a team.

Chapter 30

One week later at Angel Grove Park, Trini was busy leading another Community Fix Up. A team of scouts and volunteers were rebuilding the playground that the Griffin Pharaoh had flattened. The other Rangers were leading teams of volunteers who were filling in the crater-size footsteps created by the Megazord.

Ms. Gertrude approached Trini. "I must admit you're doing fine work here."

Trini smiled proudly. "I'm really glad you're impressed, but the thing is—" She stopped short.

Ms. Gertrude eyed Trini curiously. "Do you have something to say to me, Ms. Kwan?"

Trini took a nervous gulp before continuing. "The thing is, I spent, like, a week trying to impress you so that I could pass the leadership exam, and now I realize I should have been focusing my energy on doing what was best for the scouts."

"I see," Ms. Gertrude said with a thoughtful nod.

"Please, Trini, do continue."

Trini confidently stood up straight. "For example, at the campout the girls wanted to tell spooky stories and roast marshmallows. I thought that would be fine. Scouts do that stuff all the time. You said we couldn't, but I was leading the campout, so that should have been my decision to make."

"Interesting," Ms. Gertrude said, writing another note on her clipboard.

Trini grumbled in frustration. "As for that clipboard, would you please stop writing notes all the time? It makes me feel like you're constantly judging everything I do."

Ms. Gertrude stopped writing. "Is that all of it?"

"No! I'd also like the final score for my exam," Trini said.

Ms. Gertrude blew her whistle. The scouts hurried over and formed a line.

"As you all know, Ms. Kwan has been undergoing an examination to determine if she is suited to become an Angel Scout leader. So without further delay, here is my final assessment," Ms. Gertrude said.

Trini took a deep breath and looked at the scouts. She was thrilled to see Silvia and Daisy standing side by side, now very good friends.

Ms. Gertrude read from the notes on her clipboard. "Candidate Trini Kwan allows the scouts to participate in mischievous activities. She has a tendency to be late and offers excuses that make little sense. On numerous occasions, she simply walked away from scheduled events without explanation. This, in addition to countless errors and missteps, has resulted in a score so low that I would not dare mutter it aloud."

"So what," Silvia said.

Ms. Gertrude eyed her. "Excuse me?"

"A bunch of dumb points shouldn't decide if someone is a good leader or not," Silvia said.

The scouts all nodded in agreement.

Trini smiled at the scouts. "I appreciate what you're all trying to do, but I failed and that's nobody's fault but mine."

"You didn't let me finish," Ms. Gertrude said. "I was about to say that I do not believe points should be the final decider." She flung her clipboard away.

Trini cringed a little. "Sorry, I didn't mean to interrupt."

Ms. Gertrude cleared her throat. "In my personal

opinion, Ms. Trini Kwan is a young woman of strong moral character. She cares greatly for her community and all those who live in it. When present, her leadership skills are quite excellent. On more than one occasion, I've seen her valiantly step in to protect the scouts, even when it was simply from an actor in a mummy costume. And most importantly, Scout Leader Trini Kwan has a deep love for the Angel Scouts, equal to my own."

Trini looked at Ms. Gertrude, a little surprised. "Excuse me, Ms. Gertrude, but did you just call me 'Scout Leader'?"

"You heard me right. Congratulations, Trini," Ms. Gertrude said and extended her hand for a shake. Trini was so overjoyed, she threw her arms around Ms. Gertrude and gave her a hug. The scouts all joined in for a big group hug.

Nearby, the other Rangers were watching and applauding with pride and delight.